BEDU

Bedouin Boy, Poet King

A Profoundly Simple Journey

Colonel David W. Sutherland

U.S. Army, Retired

and

Paul McKellips

Bedu: Bedouin Boy, Poet King
by
David W. Sutherland and Paul McKellips
© 2019
All Rights Reserved
ISBN 978-1-54398-988-5 (softcover)
ISBN 978-1-54398-989-2 (eBook)

1

About 30 A.D.

BEDU WAS SITTING IN THE GREEN PASTURE NEXT TO THE POND WITH HIS SEVEN SHEEP AND FOUR GOATS. Magical words filled his thoughts while measuring the gold and pink hues of the setting sun. Flames of red and orange danced across the sky. Bedu always had words flowing through his mind.

Poetry. That's what his mother called it.

"Bedu, dinner is ready!" shouted Amira, his little sister, who disappeared around the mud and stone wall leading to the house as fast as she had arrived.

His "poetry" was shattered by a piercing voice and a stomach ready for food.

His mother Yara placed the food on a blanket in the middle of the dirt floor kitchen. Last season's leftover vegetables and fresh bone soup – from a goat they had slaughtered and devoured last month – filled the room with an inviting aroma.

"Wash up, Bedu," his mother said. Amira poured water from the vase over his hands as he gently rubbed them together over the catch basin.

The three of them stood near the food and patiently waited. Abbas finally entered, paused to admire the meal, then sat as the others quickly joined him.

"Baba, did you see the sunset?" Bedu asked his father as he pulled the bowl of soup to his lips.

"Describe it for me, Bedu. You're the poet in the family," Abbas said.

"He is not."

"Hush, Amira…let your brother speak," Yara urged as she passed the bowl of bread to her family.

"It's as though the world says goodnight. The fading rays of the sun bounce off the sea from the west, then paint themselves in different colors all over Mount Qasioun to the east. The clouds, once white and filled with rain that isn't ready to fall, reflects it all with majesty. The gold is the promise that sun will light our paths again tomorrow. The red and orange flares tell me that we'll need candles to burn until we sleep, and danger – no matter how tranquil now – always lurks nearby. And the pink reminds me of mother."

"And me?"

"And you, little sister."

Abbas smiled contently at his son. "Now I have seen the sunset, Bedu. It was majestic. You're twenty-one, son. Perhaps one day soon 'pink' will make you think of someone else?"

Yara smiled. She was hoping for a daughter-in-law but more than anything she wanted her son to be happy.

"Maybe," said Bedu. "But now I need to help you, baba. Our vegetables will soon be ready for harvest. We're out of meat again."

Abbas grimaced and looked over at his wife. She shook her head slightly, almost ashamed there wasn't anything more to serve than bone soup with some old vegetables.

"What's our count, Bedu?"

"Seven sheep...four goats."

Abbas nodded. He understood. They all understood. "Then tomorrow we will prepare one of the goats. But we need to make it last until the harvest."

Bedu's eye glanced through the open window behind his mother and up toward the mountains in the east.

"Lights," he said pointing.

"More of your sunset?" Abbas asked as he sipped his soup.

"No, baba. Burning lanterns. It looks like an army winding over the hills of Qasioun. They're just about at the split in the road."

Abbas touched Yara's shoulder as he rose to look out the window with Bedu. "I'm sure they'll split off and head down to Damascus. There's nothing they could want down this road."

"Baba...," Bedu whispered in disbelief as the army passed the road to Damascus at the split and headed toward them.

"We have an hour before they pass by. Yara, you and Amira go out to the stables and hide behind the camel. Be quiet."

Bedu leaned in closer to the window. He pointed. "Baba, one of them is riding ahead. He's coming quickly. Do you see his lantern?"

Abbas looked then gathered his thoughts. "Perhaps they mean us no harm if they're sending a rider ahead. Maybe they need directions. Bedu, go out to the road and greet the rider. Tell him how to get to Damascus."

"Yes, baba."

"And Bedu...be kind. Expect friends, not enemies."

"But baba..."

"Son, if they wanted to attack us, their horses would charge, and their lanterns would not be lit."

"What if they're marauders?"

"Then they'll quickly see that we have nothing for them to steal. Go, Bedu. Meet the rider on the road."

Bedu grabbed the lantern by the door and lit the wick that sat coiled in the oil. He ran to the road and held the lantern. The rider was still a good distance out but was moving quickly down the switchbacks of the winding dirt road out of the mountain.

Bedu was tall, but slight in build. His shoulder length hair and unshaven scruff on his face belied his youth. He was hardly a warrior and he carried no weapon other than a small blade he used when he had to cut briars away from sheep when they got entangled.

Bedu was frightened.

The horse sprinted up to his feet when the rider, dressed in flowing black silk and a black cloth tied around his forehead, pulled back on the reins. Bedu recognized the Arabian horse, the finely chiseled head, a pronounced face, the long arching neck and the height. He knew this was a horse of war.

Bedu trembled.

"Is this the home of Abbas, the shepherd boy?" the man asked as the horse pranced full circle around him in the middle of the dusty road.

Bedu could hardly speak. He was confused. "This is the home of Abbas, but he is no longer a boy. I am his son, Bedu."

The rider looked past Bedu and ahead toward the simple mud and stone hut. His eyes flared.

"I am Javad, commander of this army. Tell your father that King Melchior accepts his invitation for hospitality. His army is hungry, and we seek food and shelter for the night."

Bedu looked up to the top of Mount Qasioun. The caravan was winding through the road slowly. They appeared as a singular moving lamp of fire coming his way.

"How many men?" Bedu asked as the rider turned the horse around to head back up the mountain.

"One hundred and thirty-two," the man said as he rode away urgently.

Bedu ran back to the house. Abbas, Yara and Amira were crouching in the doorway, waiting to hear what Bedu had to say.

"What did he want?" his mother asked anxiously.

"He asked for Abbas, the shepherd boy."

"What?" Abbas struggled.

"Baba, he said King Melchior accepts your invitation for hospitality. They want food and shelter for the night."

"Baba, you know a king?" Amira asked in wonderment.

"Food? We don't have enough for ourselves, Abbas, let alone an army," Yara said.

"Bedu, get the goats and sheep into the slaughter pen. Amira, you and your mother start a large fire. We must be quick."

"How many men, Bedu? Did he say?"

"He said one hundred and thirty-two, mama. But I don't know if that includes the king or not."

Abbas and Bedu ran around the stone wall and back to the pond and stables in the hills above the house. Abbas pulled out a long leather strap and fastened it to a hook on the center beam of the stall. He reached for his three knives and began sharpening them as fast as he could. Bedu grabbed his staff and lantern and went out into the green pastures by the pond where the sheep and goats were already bedded down for the night.

"Come on…come on…get up and follow me," Bedu pleaded as he tried to lead them into the slaughtering pen. Neither the sheep nor the goats would budge.

"Son, only a *shepherd* leads the animals from the front. You must be the *butcher* tonight. You must get behind them and drive them where they do not want to go."

Bedu shook his head. "Baba, how can we do this? We'll have no more wool to sell, no more meat until the harvest, no more milk."

"Hurry, Bedu. We can't waste any time."

Bedu moved to the back of the flock. "Even Jacob's sheep, baba?"

Abbas did not answer. Bedu raised his lantern and began to yell at the goats and sheep. One by one they rose to their feet, apparently startled by the yelling and screaming of the quiet shepherd boy who had cared for them during storms and defended them from wild beasts.

By the time the caravan was close to the house, seven sheep and four goats were roasting above the large firepit. Bedu wondered if the camel and three chickens were safe or felt relieved.

The size, sound and picture of an approaching army, all riding Arabians, had even frightened Abbas as he and Yara waited in the road with lanterns. The moon was full and comingled with lantern light on the faces of more than one hundred men.

"There's a pond up here and grass for your horses," Bedu yelled as he led the way up and behind the house.

There were several wagons that were being pulled in the caravan. They, too, followed Bedu up to the pond.

Except for one.

One wagon, no fancier than the others, pulled up and stopped in front of Abbas and Yara. Amira moved closer to the strangers before Abbas pulled her back gently. A young woman got off the bench seat of the wagon and stepped down. She approached Abbas and Yara and bowed ever so slightly in respect.

"You are Abbas, the shepherd boy?" she asked.

Yara laughed. "I am Abbas, but as you can see, I am no longer a boy."

"I am Yasmin. My grandfather wishes to accept your invitation for hospitality."

An old man pushed himself up from the straw bed he was leaning against, sat up, then stood. Yasmin helped him down. The old man with white hair and flowing white beard moved closer to Abbas as a smile dashed across his face.

Abbas knew in an instant. He recognized those eyes from a night long ago. He fell to his knees and lowered his head.

"King Melchior...my family is honored." Yara and Amira were stunned to see Abbas on his knees. They quickly did the same.

"Get up, my son. I'm not a king. I told you that once before," Melchior said laughing. "Some would say a Magi, but none should say a king."

Abbas reached out for Melchior's hand and rose to his feet. They exchanged kisses on each cheek.

"King, this is my wife Yara and my daughter Amira. My son, Bedu, has led your men up to the pond and the tall grass."

Melchior looked out over the plateau as the full moon rising lit Mount Qasioun in perfect silhouette. He inhaled the aromas of the last August night.

"Something smells good, Abbas."

Abbas laughed. "A feast fit for our king."

"We have mats and pillows up around the fire and water to bathe with. Please, we are honored to have all of you with us tonight," Yara said as she started to lead them up to the fire.

Yasmin bent down to Amira. "And how old are you?" she asked with beautiful eyes twinkling in the reflections of candles and lanterns.

"I'm eleven. How old are you?" Amira asked.

"Amira!" her father scolded as Melchior laughed heartily.

"I'm nineteen, Amira. I am so happy to see another girl." Amira took Yasmin's hand and they followed behind Yara to the pond.

Melchior took the arm of Abbas and they walked slowly behind.

"You remember me?" the old man asked.

"I could never forget you. It was the most amazing night of my life."

"You were so young."

"Yes, I was but seventeen…a boy…that was thirty years ago," Abbas reflected. "I have always wondered if you were still living."

"Well, I'm ninety-two now. No plans to go anytime soon." They laughed. "Did you tell your family about that night?"

Abbas stopped. He looked down, almost as if he was ashamed. "No."

Melchior patted him on the back. "Then tonight we will."

The king's army sat around the fire pit as the flames started to die and the embers glowed. Amira walked in and out of the army with a wash basin for them to clean their hands after the feast. No one had hunger anymore.

Bedu sat off to the side, away from the others. He was brooding, almost angry. An entire army of strange men had emptied his father's house of livestock. They would soon be gone, and his family would have no wool to sell, no meat to eat, and no flock to tend to. "A king should know better than to take everything that a simple man has," Bedu reasoned.

The old man rose to his feet and the din of conversation settled to silence. All wanted to hear what the king had to say, maybe even Bedu.

"I have spent my life studying the stars," Melchior said as he turned his eyes to the heavens. "The light of the moon blocks most of what the stars are saying tonight, but such was not the case thirty years ago when I met Abbas, the shepherd boy."

Bedu perked up. Amira edged closer to the king.

"There was an unusual star rising in the morning western sky. I had never seen such a thing. It was most definitely a sign. It meant something to me. I see things before other people see them. That's why they call me their leader. Leaders see things earlier. But I'm not a king."

The entire army laughed then quieted down.

"I set off from Persia, on a camel, by myself. I was going to follow that star. I had to. It was calling me. I brought gold…a gift… for whomever that star would reveal. On the outskirts of Babylon, I met Gaspar. He had traveled from the east, a place I had never even heard of. He, too, was following that star. His skin was darker than any I had ever seen before. He brought a resin for perfumes and incense. It was to be a gift, as well, for whomever the star would reveal."

Bedu moved in closer, just behind the last circle of warriors.

"Gaspar and I rode in near silence for more than eleven days. I did not speak his language nor he mine. But the star spoke to both of us and we understood. We woke one morning in Moab. There we met Balthasar. He had traveled from Arabia and he, too, was following the star. Balthasar had myrrh. Oh my. *Myrrh*. The aroma from the perfume was from the gods. A small wound healed quickly just at its touch."

"What did the star mean?" Amira asked as Yara quieted her down. Yasmin was just as captivated by the story as her new friend was.

"That a king was to be born. Gaspar, Balthasar and I stopped to visit the sitting king. He was not happy when we told him about the star. So, we continued and finally, there in Bethlehem of Judea, our journey ended."

Abbas rose and stood next to King Melchior. Bedu saw him glance at Yara with almost an apology in his eyes.

"My father had asked me to go on a journey, to travel down to Hebron. There I would find a tribe of my cousins – Bedouins – who were breeding Jacob's sheep. My father only wanted the best sheep, and Hebron offered the best in the region."

"How long was your journey, baba?" Bedu asked from the back of the crowd.

"Nineteen days to Hebron, Bedu, nineteen days. I purchased three sheep with the shekels my father gave me and started to lead them home. Two ewes and one ram. We hoped they would give us a large flock. The first night coming home was short. I was so weary, and the sheep were moving slowly. So, I camped for the night in the fields near Bethlehem with several other shepherds. We weren't in the village itself, but right near the stables where all of the other livestock stayed."

"What happened, baba?" Amira asked as Yasmin pulled her closer.

"I'm not sure," Abbas paused. "Maybe a dream…maybe something else. I woke up surrounded by light, in the middle of a very dark night. Just stars. One star was very bright and low in the sky, but there was no moon. Not that night."

"Were you afraid?" Yasmin asked.

"Frightened beyond belief. Then I heard it."

"Heard what?" Bedu asked.

"A voice. A voice from the light told me not to be afraid. The voice said it was good news."

"Gaspar, Balthasar and I gave our gifts and paid our respects. It was time to go home, but we were weary, too. And hungry!" King Melchior said with a great laugh.

"My grandfather is always hungry," Yasmin chimed in.

"As we passed by the stables and headed out to the road through the fields, we came across Abbas, the shepherd boy. He was the only one still awake and he was pacing back and forth. He had just lit his fire."

"I couldn't sleep after that dream...or whatever it was."

"The three of us got down and shared the fire with Abbas. Soon the other shepherds stirred and joined us. By now, we were all hungry. We never asked him to, but Abbas led his animals away and before we knew it, we were having a feast beneath a special star, a meal fit for three kings. But I'm *not* a king," Melchior laughed.

"What about your sheep, baba? Your father gave you money to buy sheep...breeding stock. And you went home with nothing? Not even the shekels he had given you?" Bedu asked as he moved in closer.

"Yes, I was worried. My father would be very disappointed with me. The next day, I started the journey home from Bethlehem on the road to Damascus. This time I followed the path along the Jordan River. When I went over Mount Nebo, I spotted a stray sheep, tangled in the briars. There was no flock and no shepherd in sight. She was lost. So, I freed her and carried her down the hills until we were on lower ground. She was a Jacob's sheep. Mount Hermon was much taller. I camped on the side of the mountain that night. I awoke early in the morning to the sound of my one sheep bleating. And there in the distance was another sheep, another ewe. She was alone, by herself and frightened. Now, I had two sheep. Two days past the Sea of Galilee, I spotted another stray sheep. She had fallen into a small canyon. Her leg was broken. I wrapped it up as tight as I could, and I carried her all the way home to Damascus."

"How many days did you carry her, Abbas?" Yara asked.

"Three more days."

"Did you tell your father the story?" Bedu asked.

Abbas and Melchior exchanged glances. "My father got three ewes for the shekels he paid, but no ram. I thought it best not to explain the *whole* story."

Everyone laughed as Abbas sat down. "Abbas forgot to mention one important thing. When we were about to leave our camp the next morning, I realized that all the other sheep belonged to the other shepherds who had already left. Abbas gave us *everything* he had. Nothing was left. Not even his shekels. Despite that, Abbas - the shepherd boy with nothing left to his name – invited me to share his hospitality again…if ever I was traveling near Damascus. And now, thirty years later, here we sit."

King Melchior sat down.

Bedu was struck with the thought of history repeating itself. Thanks to his hospitality, his father once again had nothing. Bedu stood and walked behind the army as everyone enjoyed conversation and full stomachs. Yara, Amira and Yasmin were deep in conversation as King Melchior and Abbas discussed the king's most recent journey.

Bedu looked in and out of the wagons. There were fine linens, collectibles, bags of grain and clothing. One of the wagons carried four old and dusty trunks. They were closed. He looked around. No one else was looking. Bedu opened the first trunk and quickly stepped back in awe. The trunk was filled to the top with gold coins. He opened the second. More coins. The third and fourth were full too. There was too much gold to count. King Melchior could not possibly have any idea how much gold he had. Surely, he was a king to have that much fortune.

Bedu looked around again. No one was watching. He reached into the closest trunk and pulled out five gold coins and stuffed them in his satchel. "This should pay for what baba lost tonight," Bedu reasoned.

Javad stepped out of the shadows of the stable, behind the camel, and watched as Bedu walked quickly away and sat down next to his father.

"How far have you traveled on this journey?" Abbas asked.

"From Susa to Babylon then up to Ninevah, across Assyria on the Silk Road then here to Damascus. We're going to Bsharri for Yasmin, then on to Aabdeh for me. I want a house overlooking the sea."

"Bsharri? The cedars of God. It's only a five-day ride from here, but I have never seen the cedars," Abbas said sadly.

"My granddaughter's dream. Yasmin wants to live among the cedars and spend her life there. She's stubborn and determined like her father was."

"Your son?" asked Bedu.

"Yes, he was a warrior, a commander in the Parthian Empire. Civil wars are always unfolding in Persia. It's an ongoing struggle for power. They were ambushed one night as they slept. My son woke first as he was at the front of the encampment. He fought off an invading army by himself, well, at least long enough until his men could wake and defend themselves. Only one man died that night, and one hundred and thirty-two lived."

"Yasmin's father?" Abbas asked.

The old man nodded. "I've been taking care of Yasmin ever since. Her mother died in childbirth. And now, wherever I go, his army takes me. Sometimes it's annoying," King Melchior said smiling as some of the warriors nearby laughed. "They will build a home for Yasmin in the cedars. Too cold for me there in the winter, though I do enjoy seeing snow. I'll keep going to Aabdeh in the Kingdom of Armenia. It's time to retire and just look at the stars hanging out over the sea."

"Yasmin is going to live in Bsharri? By herself?" Bedu asked with more interest.

"She has no husband, not yet anyway. She has an army of would-be suitors but has no interest in warriors. I'm tired of war, too. This is her dream. This is who she is. Your father says you're a poet, Bedu. Is that correct?"

Bedu shrugged his shoulders in embarrassment. "Oh no...not really. I mean, I like to put words to things I see, and feel...or think. But that's all."

Yasmin perked up and looked over at Bedu.

"What do you see now, Bedu? What do you feel? What are you thinking?"

Bedu paused. He shook his head contritely.

"Nothing really."

"Look to the heavens...see the army gathered around you. What do you feel?"

Bedu dropped his head. He searched for words. Then slowly, he began to speak. "From something...we become nothing; and from nothing...we become something. Dusty footsteps on winding roads of mud and stone lead to something, yet quickly leave nothing behind. When the sun rises, will seeds once planted rise for the harvest? Or must we wait another day? Why can't we enjoy today that which we planted only yesterday? Patience. Like the deep roots of a cedar tree that once blew in the wind as but a seed, patience brings us the strength of the trunk for our families and the shade of the branches to cover our worry. From the heights of great cedars, will we look back at dirty footsteps and realize that nothing…was ever left behind."

Silence filled the camp.

"That was stupid," Amira finally said before Yara tapped her on the head. "Sorry, but it was," she whispered.

Javad walked up to King Melchior, bent down, and whispered in his ear. The old man closed his eyes then looked over at Bedu.

"That was wonderful. Thank you. Javad reminds me that it is time to get our sleep. We have a long journey tomorrow."

Everyone stood and stretched and started to make their ways to slumber. Yasmin said goodnight to Amira as she and Yara walked to the house.

"Bedu, I would like to speak with you in the morning if I may…before we head out," the king said.

The boy nodded. "Did he know? How could he know? Did the rider see me?" A million thoughts and the heavy weight of guilt raced through Bedu's mind. His father would be so disappointed.

Bedu tossed and turned all night. His stomach was upset, and his head felt full and throbbing. At the first hint of morning light, he sprang up from his bedroll and walked to the pond and the green pasture. It was his morning routine. Then he remembered.

The sheep and the goats were gone.

The army was hitching up wagons and packing their bedding. He saw his father talking to King Melchior as he helped the old man up and into his wagon. He figured his father already knew. Bedu went back into the house and got his satchel. He anticipated what might be coming next.

As he walked up to King Melchior's wagon, Abbas stepped back and moved away.

"Your father and I have had a talk. We both agree. I need something from you."

"I understand," Bedu said softly with his head bowed in shame. He reached for his satchel. "I don't know what -."

"Two things actually," King Melchior interrupted. "First, I'm asking you to go to Bsharri this winter and check on Yasmin. These men will be heading back to Persia after they build her house and get me settled in the Kingdom of Armenia. I don't know who else to ask. I hope you are willing."

Bedu was shocked. It was not at all what he was expecting.

"And the second thing."

"Here it comes," Bedu thought.

King Melchior reached out his hand toward Bedu and opened his palm.

"I want to give you five gold coins. Take these coins and travel the path of your father along the Jordan River, past Bethlehem and into Hebron. I'm told it's there that you will find seven of the best of Jacob's sheep and at least four goats. Maybe you can pay for more. Bring them home to your family, Bedu."

"Magi, that's too much," Abbas protested. "He can buy a small herd with that many coins."

The boy felt sick. "Does he not know I already stole five pieces of his gold?" Bedu's thoughts ran through his confused mind.

"But –."

King Melchior raised his hand. "I have spent my whole life watching the stars, my son. They tell me things. They speak to me. As you travel the path of your father, I want you to pay attention to the seven stars of Pleiades. The Greeks called them the seven sisters, the daughters of Atlas who hold up the night sky. Each one of the stars will tell you something, Bedu. They will have meaning for you. Don't miss it."

Bedu wiped the tears from his cheek. "What kind of meaning?"

"Who you *were*...who you *are*...who you will forever *be*."

Bedu tried to laugh. "I already know all of that. I am Bedu, the Bedouin boy from Damascus who guides sheep."

"No, son...that's what you *do*. This journey will tell you who you *are* which is far more important than what you do."

Bedu nodded as Yasmin climbed up into the seat of the wagon.

"I liked your poem, Bedu. I liked it a lot," she said as Bedu blushed and turned away.

"One last thing, Bedu. The seventh star can be difficult to see. Look closely. You'll find it. And then, when your journey is over, come find me. I want to hear all about your discoveries."

"Have *you* seen the seventh star, King Melchior?" Bedu asked.

"Yes. I have good eyes. I'm told there's an eighth, but that star still alludes me. Perhaps in Aabdeh."

Javad rode to the front of the caravan and with a signal, one hundred and thirty-two soldiers, several wagons, an old king, and a beautiful young granddaughter, left dusty footprints on the road to Bsharri to find the cedars of God.

A FEW DAYS later, Abbas, Yara and Amira stood outside the house. Yara was in tears and hugging her only son, Bedu. His satchel was packed with enough small pieces of bread and dried meat leftover from the feast to last him a few days. His staff was in his hand and a small bladed knife beneath his belt draw.

"Are you clear on the directions, son?" Abbas asked for the tenth time.

"Yes, baba, a nineteen-day walk to Hebron and thirty-six to bring the flock home. I'll be home in early November. I'll head through the Golan, to the Sea of Galilee, then follow the Jordan River south, then west past Jericho, then through Jerusalem, around Bethlehem – the land of King David – and then straight to Hebron, the land of Abraham. I'll be fine, baba."

"The Hasbani, Dan and Baniyas flow into the Jordan, through the Sea of Galilee and out to the Dead Sea. If you get to the Dead Sea you've gone too far. You must go west before you reach the Dead Sea."

"Yes, baba, you told me."

"When you get to Hebron, find the shepherd Wali. He is our cousin. You are part of his tribe. He will know me. He will sell you the animals from his stock."

"You have the five gold coins?" Yara asked.

"Yes, mama," though Bedu knew he was carrying ten, he could not tell them what a terrible thing he had done. "Baba, how much will I have to pay for the animals?"

"I don't know. Depends what the moneychangers tell you. But you should be able to replace our flock with one coin, maybe two."

"I will bring the remainder back to you, baba, I promise. Mama, I won't be home for the harvest. Make sure we have a vegetable feast when I return," Bedu said as he kissed his mother's cheeks and stroked the top of Amira's head.

With that, Bedu took off walking. Every few minutes he turned and waived back to the family who stood frozen in time by the house. They finally disappeared in the horizon as Bedu's dusty footprints headed toward the sea and away from the rising sun before a sharp turn and a long trek south into Judea.

2

EDU TOOK THE SHEPHERD'S TRAIL OVER THE MOUNTAINS AND DOWN INTO THE GOLAN HEIGHTS. The weather was perfect in late summer, and it only took him one-and-a-half days to reach the eastern slopes of Mount Hermon.

From what Bedu could tell, the Sea of Galilee looked beautiful, peaceful and calm. From the side of the hills he could see many boats, perhaps fishermen he thought.

Nine days past the southern tip of Galilee, rain started to fall. At first it was gentle and soothing. Bedu captured the rain drops on large grape leaves. It was refreshing. His sandals started to slip on the wet trail. There was no break in the clouds, so he decided to build a shelter under the trees out of branches and palm leaves for the night. Hopefully the sun would return in the morning.

The morning brought more rain, only harder. He looked over at the Jordan River which was moving faster now. The brown mud on the bottom was making its presence known on the top of the water. It would be a wet day of walking, but he knew he must continue.

The next two days the rain fell even harder. The Jordan was raging with anger and the boundaries of the river were lapping up against his trail. He was grateful that he didn't have seven sheep and four goats to protect now.

He approached a small village. The rain was falling in torrents. The river had risen far above the banks and was now driving through the town. He heard the screams of a woman and saw six men run past him to the first house. Bedu ran after them with staff in hand and a satchel heavy with water and ten gold coins.

"My son, my son…my child is in there," the woman screamed as the Jordan River started to flow through her house. The water was already up to her shoulders.

The men pulled her back though she tried to fight them. She broke free and dove into the water. One man grabbed her foot and pulled her back to the stone wall they each stood on.

They watched. There was nothing to do but watch.

Bedu ran to the house. The water was up to his waist and rising quickly. The men and the screaming mother stood on the wall watching helplessly. Bedu dove into the water. He opened his eyes but through the mud of the Jordan River he could see nothing. Then he felt something.

He felt another hand.

"Please help me," Bedu pleaded with the men on the wall. "I can feel his hand. His clothing is stuck but I can free him. Hold my feet so the river doesn't carry me away too."

The men jumped into the water. Two on each side and one on each foot. Bedu pulled his satchel off and handed it to the mother.

With staff in hand, Bedu returned to the bottom of the water. He felt where the boy's robe was caught around the cooking rocks. He reached for the boy's hand but could no longer find it. He tore the child's robe away from the jagged rock and grabbed a foot before the current could carry the boy deeper into the house. With the hook of his staff, he reached out and wrapped it around the boy's shoulder and pulled him close. The men could see that Bedu had the boy and together they pulled them both to higher ground.

The boy was lifeless.

His mother started to scream and wail in anguish. She rocked back and forth, hitting her chest and face.

Bedu carried the boy to the dry ground in front of the next house and rolled him on his side. Bedu kept pushing on the boy's chest.

"Come on, come on…you can do this," Bedu urged the child as six others and an anguished mother watched.

Suddenly, the Jordan River poured out of the young boy's mouth as he gasped for air. He screamed and cried in panic as his mother burst into tears of joy. She held her son close to her chest and rocked him as the Jordan raged behind her.

"I have never seen anything like that," one man said in astonishment.

"How did you know what to do?" asked another.

Bedu picked up his satchel and pulled the leather strap over his neck and one shoulder. "I could not have done it without *all* of you. Thank you. You see, I'm a shepherd. I've had more than one sheep who has wandered off and found trouble. But each one is worth saving."

The woman fell to her feet and kissed Bedu's muddy and wet sandals. He was embarrassed.

"You have given me my child back," she said through tears.

"It wasn't just me. If it were not for these six men, I could not have done this alone. The river was too powerful. But all of us – together – we did what just one could not do."

"Where are you headed, shepherd?" one asked.

"What shepherd has no sheep?" another asked.

"I'm going to Jericho, then south to Hebron where I will buy more sheep and restore my father's flock," Bedu said as the rain calmed down.

"Jericho is right down this road. You'll be there in an hour, before sunset…if the road hasn't washed out."

Bedu laughed, touched the cheek of the boy, and headed toward Jericho.

He found a dry place to camp outside of Jericho. The angry clouds had subsided and there were breaks in the sky. He laid back and stared at the heavens. He thought about his journey, the rain, the raging Jordan River, and a little boy whose robe was stuck on a rock.

It was an amazing day.

Bedu's eyes pulled his thoughts away from the day. He noticed that one star seemed brighter than all the others. He pushed himself up on his elbows and focused.

"King Melchior?" he whispered. With a satisfied smile, Bedu fell into a deep sleep.

Collaborate: *Work together as a team and transform the impossible, to the possible.*

3

I T TOOK TWO DAYS TO WALK TO JERUSALEM. If he hurried – and no more rain fell – he could get to Hebron in three more, as planned.

When he passed the outskirts of Bethlehem, he couldn't help but remember the story told by his father, Abbas, and King Melchior. He could only imagine how frightened his father must've been. "It was probably a dream, just like baba said," he thought.

Bedu was still full of energy from the flood. He wanted to see the look on his own mother's face when he told her all about it.

Efrat was about halfway between Jerusalem and Hebron. It was still too early to camp for the night. The road seemed well-traveled but not as many trees and places to camp. So, he decided to push the fading daylight until he could find adequate cover.

There was some traffic on the road, but not much. Even less as night pushed in to replace the day.

The last thing Bedu remembered seeing was the tiny patch of trees around the bend in the road. He had thought it would make a fine shelter. That was before a hand holding a rock came crashing down against his head above his right ear.

Bedu awoke to the feeling of a wet cloth on his head. He opened his eyes haltingly as bright sun coming through an open window was more than painful to look at. He saw the face of a woman in front of his and behind her a man. He was smiling.

"Welcome back," the man said. "You've been sleeping for three days."

The woman pulled the cloth back from Bedu's face.

"You must be hungry," she said.

Bedu nodded.

"You were robbed on the road to Efrat three nights ago. I found you the next morning on the side of the road, bleeding and in pretty bad shape."

"Where am I?" Bedu asked, though each word was a struggle. The light was blinding.

"You're in our home. You're safe here. We will take care of you until you're ready to travel again. Where are you from, son?"

"Damascus."

"Damascus?" the woman answered as she prepared some soup for her patient.

"Why that's two weeks north of here. What are you doing in Efrat?" the man asked.

"I'm going to Hebron...to buy more sheep and goats...to restore my father's flock."

The man and the woman exchanged uncomfortable glances.

"My satchel?" Bedu asked though he already knew the answer.

"There was no satchel, son. All I saw was the bloody robe you're wearing now and your staff."

Bedu closed his eyes. The pain had found a new target right in his old satchel. His mind was overcome with failure and guilt as his head throbbed harder in pain.

The soup helped. Bedu sat up and ate two bowls while he told them about King Melchior, the Persian army and Abbas, the shepherd boy. He also told them about his father's dream in Bethlehem and saving a boy inside a house near Jericho, a house that had become the Jordan River.

They laughed. Bedu realized they weren't too sure about his tall tales.

"You've taken a good hit on the head, son. You may have some crazy thoughts in your head for a few days, but it'll get better," the man said.

"Bedu…my name is Bedu."

"Welcome Bedu…you may stay as long as you need to. I'm sure your mother would do the same for our son were he in such a situation," the woman said.

Bedu smiled. He knew she was right. Mothers are always right about those kinds of things.

"When you feel better, Bedu, I could use some help with our fence. I can't pay you much. That is, if you want some work."

Bedu thought about it. Looking at their house, he knew they were simple people. The man was perhaps a shepherd too, just like his own father. There was no way they could pay him ten gold coins, but anything would be better than the nothing Bedu now had.

"I would like that."

Bedu stayed two weeks. He rebuilt the man's rock wall from corner to corner. They were both amazed at how much he could do with only the rocks and mud around their house. Bedu even walked out into fields nearby and carried more rocks back, stone by stone. He built a swinging gate so their sheep and chickens could be secure from other animals looking for a quick meal.

The morning meal was over, the wall was rebuilt, and his wounds had healed, though not his pride. Bedu knew it was time to leave. He thought about heading home but hated the thought of facing his father with no sheep, no goats and no gold coins.

"I can never thank you enough for your care and understanding. I must leave today," Bedu said as he smiled at his hosts.

The man stood up quickly and left for the back of the house.

"Where will you go, Bedu?" the woman asked.

"I'll continue on to Hebron. I have cousins there from my tribe. My father wants to buy some of their sheep."

The man reappeared in the dirt-floored kitchen as Bedu and the woman stood. "It's not much, but I appreciate what you did. The wall is perfect. Please take these three shekels of silver. Perhaps it will help you buy a sheep or two."

The man reached out and dropped the three coins in Bedu's hand. With fingers clasped, he touched his heart in thanks as a tear streamed down his face. The woman wiped it away as a huge smile dashed across her face.

"I don't know what the other one looked like, but I sewed you a new satchel."

The new satchel was so much nicer than the cloth and leather one he had before.

"It's from sheepskin...very soft to the touch and durable. I hope you like it." Tears poured from Bedu's eyes. He had never seen such kindness from complete strangers, strangers that weren't even part of his tribe. The man didn't need to stop. The woman didn't need to nurse him back to health or feed him meals. They didn't need to give him work or pay him with three shekels of silver. And she didn't need to make him a new satchel.

"And here's an extra bedroll. You'll need it, Bedu," she said.

"I hope one day we will meet Bedu, the shepherd boy from Damascus, again," the man said as Bedu walked to the door, then along a new stone wall, and out through a swinging gate. He turned, looked and waved back several times to the couple who stood watching in the doorway, seemingly frozen in time.

By the time he reached Halhul he had a decision to make. Hebron was only a few more hours away, but he could not make it there before nightfall.

He hadn't enjoyed much luck traveling at night.

There were plenty of places to sleep outside the village, but he was worried. The village gates to Halhul were closed yet there were women and children camped outside the gate. They were all covered with sores.

They were outcasts.

Bedu needed to sleep but he was afraid. "What if they're sick? What if I catch their disease? I could die," Bedu thought to himself.

He found a tree and unfolded the bedroll the woman had given him. He placed the satchel under his back and held the staff across his chest so no one would bother him.

A woman started to walk over. Her two children tagged along behind. He closed his eyes slightly but peeked with one just in time to see she was coming straight for him. The sores were all over her face and hands. He turned his face and closed his eyes completely so he couldn't see her.

Perhaps she would think he had already fallen asleep and didn't want to be bothered.

"Please, boy, do you have food? My children have not eaten for days."

Bedu remained still. His eyes were closed.

"Please, boy, only food for my children…not me."

Bedu pretended to sleep.

Finally, the woman turned, started to cry softly, and led her children back to the gates of Halhul.

Bedu opened his eyes. She was gone. "Good," he thought.

The smell of food cooking wafted over the walls from the village. The aroma was pleasing. Bedu looked up to the sky. Magical, but sad words filled his thoughts while measuring the gold and pink hues of a setting sun. Flames of red and orange danced across the sky.

"Who you *were*…who you *are*…who you will *be*." The words of King Melchior were the only words he could hear.

Bedu jumped to his feet. He folded up his bedroll, put the satchel around his head and shoulder, and gathered up his staff. He marched over to the gate. The tender asked to see his hands and arms.

He was clean.

The gate was opened and Bedu entered Halhul. He could see the vendor who was cooking lamb kabobs on the side of the road by the merchant's store. Bedu walked over. The man's rock stove had more than twenty kabobs that were almost fully cooked above the hot coals.

"How much for all of your kabobs?" Bedu asked.

"You must be very hungry," the man laughed. "Three shekels." The man turned away knowing that Bedu probably didn't have the appetite for three shekels of silver, let alone twenty kabobs.

Bedu reached into his new satchel and pulled out his only three silver coins from the hidden pocket. "Give me all of them."

The man was surprised. He laid out a piece of cloth and put twenty kabobs on it and rolled it back up. Bedu handed him his money and returned to the gate which was quickly opened for him by the tender.

He walked over to the woman who had approached him. She was sitting in the dirt with her head buried in her hands.

Bedu unrolled the cloth as she looked up. The aroma of the kabobs focused her attention. Bedu reached out and gave her a kabob. She grabbed it carefully from the stick protruding from the other side, so as not to touch him. Then he pulled one out each for her children. They were careful too.

The other outcasts around saw what Bedu was doing as they got up and edged closer.

Everyone – all twenty outcasts – got a lamb kabob from Bedu, the shepherd boy from Damascus. There was no more crying. The outcasts gathered together and enjoyed an unexpected feast.

Bedu went back to the same tree and unfolded his bedroll. He placed the now empty satchel beneath his back again and laid the staff across his chest. His eyes focused on the heavens.

Two stars seemed brighter than all the others in the sky. He thought of King Melchior.

He had lost everything on the road to Efrat. Yet, complete strangers took him in and restored his health. He turned his face and tried not to see the outcasts in Halhul, but Efrat had opened the eyes of his heart to a new understanding.

He was willing to give up the only money he had left, money he had earned, to meet the needs of those who needed a stranger's mercy, too.

The morning sun stirred, Bedu. He opened his eyes and was immediately scared.

He was surrounded by the outcasts he had fed the night before. The woman was already awake.

"We gathered around you last night, a circle of protection. I hope you don't mind. But no one will be willing to attack you, or rob you, if you are surrounded by people like us."

Understanding: *Realize you're not alone. Have empathy for those in need and turn nothing into something.*

4

I T WAS ALREADY NOVEMBER. His family would be expecting him next week.

He had promised King Melchior that he would travel to Bsharri in the winter and check in on his granddaughter, Yasmin. But Bedu had just arrived in Hebron. He had no money. He had no sheep. He had no goats. And now he needed to find a cousin named Wali.

Bedu saw a merchant shop in the middle of town. The merchant sold grains, breads, and even some woven baskets. There were several customers in the store when he entered. When the merchant finished selling bread, he looked over at Bedu. His robe was soiled, dirty and stained from old blood that never washed out. The staff was a clear giveaway.

"Shepherd boy! Are you shopping or stealing?" the merchant asked gruffly.

"I am from Damascus," Bedu stuttered.

"Then you're a long way from home."

"I am looking for one who is called Wali. He is my cousin, part of my tribe."

The merchant nodded his head and pointed. "Two roads over, then right. Big farm. But Wali is in mourning right now. You just missed the funeral."

"Funeral?" Bedu managed to ask.

"His youngest son…and his wife. They both caught the fever. But not Noam. He's fine."

"Noam?"

"Their only son. I don't know what Wali is going to do. His wife is gone and he's too old to care for the little boy. Wali's three other sons are much older, live in other towns, and have full families of their own," the merchant said.

Bedu thanked him for the information then walked down past two roads, then right.

It was a big farm. The field behind the house was filled with dozens of ewes and another pen held several rams. No one was around. A black scarf hung across the front door.

Bedu walked through the stone and mud wall leading up to the front of the house. The door was closed. He knocked softly.

No answer.

He knocked louder.

Still nothing.

"Who are *you*?" a young voice asked from across the front porch. Bedu could see a little boy in a blue robe playing with sticks and a piece of cloth.

"I am Bedu. Are you Noam?"

The boy nodded as the front door finally opened. A weary and tired looking man stared straight into Bedu's eyes. He appeared irritated that a stranger might be on his porch speaking with his grandson without an invitation.

"Go away. I'm in mourning," the man said as he started to close the door.

"I am your cousin. My father is Abbas, a shepherd from Damascus," Bedu said urgently before the door could close.

"Abbas?"

Bedu nodded. "He sent me to find Wali."

Wali opened the door and motioned for Bedu to come in. Noam followed quickly behind. Hot water was still on the rocks. Wali poured two cups of chai and invited Bedu to sit. Noam sat next to his new cousin.

"Now is not a good time for me, Bedu. I just lost my youngest son and his wife. Noam is now my responsibility."

"I'm sorry, baba, I know you must be in pain with a broken heart. Perhaps I can help you for a few days with your flock and with Noam. I am a good shepherd. I can help."

Wali was silent for several minutes as they drank their tea.

"Why did Abbas send you all the way down to Hebron? Does he need more sheep?" Wali finally asked.

Bedu nodded. "Yes, baba, he sent me down with money to buy seven of Jacob's sheep and four goats. He said you have the best sheep in all of Judea."

Wali allowed a half-smile to break across his lips. It was his first smile after three days of mourning.

"I only met Abbas once, maybe thirty years ago. He came to buy sheep from my father. Pick the ones you want out back. We can agree on a price."

Bedu pawed at the dirt on the floor with his sandal. He didn't know what to say or where to start.

"You have money, don't you?" Wali finally asked.

"I did, baba, I truly did. But I was robbed on the road to Efrat and I lost everything."

"So how are you going to buy sheep and goats from me?"

"I could work for you. I can tend your flock and you can pay me with sheep and goats. You determine the price of my work," Bedu suggested, now almost pleading.

"I have sons for that work," Wali dismissed.

"But they don't live here anymore, baba," Noam chimed in. "They have already left and gone to their own homes with their own families."

Wali was silent. Bedu could tell he was thinking it over.

"Okay. But my sheep are not free. I'm not going to pay for work in advance and then just let you run home. You sound like my youngest son. He wanted to *talk* about work without really *doing* the work, yet he was first in line to enjoy the sheep's cheese, the drinking milk, and sell the wool. That's not how you do it, Bedu. There's no future in that. That's not a business. If you live life that way, in thirty more years you'll be sending your own son down to buy more sheep from Noam."

Bedu heard his words carefully. Wali was talking about something much greater than he had ever imagined.

"What is it that you can teach me, baba?"

"How to breed sheep. How to build a business. You can stay the winter, but *only* if you are willing to learn how to breed sheep."

"Your other sons...they do this?" Bedu asked.

"Very well, in fact. They are each successful. My wife even taught their wives."

"Taught their wives how to breed sheep?"

Wali laughed. "No, how to weave their wool into garments. You see, Bedu, if you just sell the wool you earn one price. But if you weave your own wool into beautiful garments you can earn a far greater price."

Bedu thought about Wali's words carefully. "There is much I need to tell you, baba, about King Melchior and his granddaughter Yasmin. But my father is expecting me to be home *next* week."

"Well, that's not going to happen, Bedu. It's impossible. You can stay the winter and learn what I must teach you, or you can head out the door and start walking home. It's your choice."

Noam looked up into Bedu's eyes and smiled. "Want to play, Bedu?"

Bedu smiled back.

"Yes, I do. Baba, I will spend the winter with you and learn all that you can teach me."

Wali held out his hand and Bedu responded. The handshake was the start of a new venture for Bedu.

"You two go out and play. I will prepare a meal."

Noam bolted to his feet and Bedu rose right behind him.

"Bedu...we start with the sunrise. Tomorrow my days of mourning shall end."

Bedu was the first to awake in the morning. He folded up his bedroll just as Noam's eyes opened. Wali was still asleep in his bedroom.

"Want to see the horses?" Noam whispered.

Bedu nodded. They both snuck out of the house without a sound.

The corral was filled with dozens of ewes and the adjacent pen had at least six rams. They appeared to be about the same ages, Bedu thought.

"This way," Noam said as he ran around the wooden wall at the edge of the stables.

Bedu stopped in sheer awe.

"Two? Two black Arabians? They are beautiful."

"One was my father's, the other belongs to my grandfather."

Wali walked out and around the corner of the stables.

"Good morning, baba," Bedu said as Noam ran to his grandfather's side and hugged him. Wali bent down so Noam could kiss him on both cheeks.

"I guess I will sell my son's horse. He's young, but far too much spirit for me. I can't handle him. Do you have horses, Bedu?"

"No. Just goats and sheep, well, we used to...and some chickens and a camel."

"Do you know why?"

Bedu shook his head. "Because you only operate a farm for your own use. You have never thought bigger than your own needs. If you build a business, you will have an endless supply of the things you need, and so will the villages and people around you."

"Sell him to me, baba," Bedu said unexpectedly.

Wali laughed. "Sell my Arabian to a shepherd boy from Damascus who has no money?"

"That's not quite right, baba. The shepherd boy is building a business. This will be the first of many horses he buys."

Noam look at his grandfather with eager expectation. Wali nodded his head.

"Alright, alright…I think you're getting it. I will grant you a line of credit. The horse is yours, but you will start to pay off your credit by caring for both horses."

Bedu reached out his hand first this time.

"And all of the sheep and goats," Wali added as everyone laughed and hugged.

"Does he have a name?" Bedu asked.

"My son called him Atlas. At night you can see his daughters, the seven sisters who hold up the sky, or so they say. Pleiades, I think that's what they call it."

Bedu bent down to Noam. "Do *you* work yet?"

"I like playing better," Noam answered.

"I like playing, too, But, when I was seven, my father taught me to work as well. How would you like to work for me? I'm going to need help tending thirty ewes, six rams and two Arabians."

"Thirty-five ewes," Wali added proudly.

"Are you going to pay me?" Noam asked.

"Of course. I'm running a business now."

"Okay. But can we start after breakfast? I'm hungry."

They all walked back to the house for the morning meal.

After breakfast, Wali led Bedu out to the holding pen where the six rams roamed freely. Wali walked over to each and inspected them individually as only a doting father might do over his young sons.

"Early November is the perfect time to breed in Hebron, "Wali said. "The ewe's fertility increases as the length of the days decrease. With shorter days, they go into heat every two weeks or so."

"Heat?" Bedu asked. Wali laughed.

"These are all good rams with a great breeding history."

"How do you know that, baba?"

"Because they're mine and I have bred them before. But if you are buying one from a stranger, you must ask. Always buy three or four rams at a time. You never really know until later."

"How much later?"

"Oh, about five months or so…March, early April. That's when an ewe's pregnancy ends, and lambs are born."

Bedu grew anxious. "March or April?" he thought. "That's *much* longer than just the winter."

Wali led Bedu out of the rams' pen and over to the open field where the ewes were grazing behind the corral.

"I know that almost half of the flock are of good breeding stock. Twenty of them produced lambs last April."

"But you have thirty-five now," Bedu added.

"Yes. The ones that didn't produce last year were sold to shepherd boys from Damascus who didn't know any better. They just wanted cheese, milk and wool for their own use. The others – the ones that produced – were sold to shepherds who knew what they were talking about."

"They had a business," Bedu said confidently.

"Yes, they did. If you buy rams from a shepherd, just know that he probably fed them grains to fatten them up for sale. As soon as you get rams, get them on fresh grain and the best hay you can buy."

"Why?"

"He'll produce strong and healthy lambs."

"When do you put the rams and ewes together?" Bedu asked.

Wali scoured through the herd until he found the one he wanted and led Bedu over. Wali used his staff and guided one ewe away from the others.

"She's in heat?"

"Maybe. She's waving her tail a lot. But the ram will let us know."

Wali opened the pen and let one ram come out. He was curious and walked around the ewe.

"She's peeing, grandfather!" Noam yelled as he ran up closer.

Wali smiled. "Now watch the ram. When the ewe relieves herself, the ram will sniff it. If he puts his leg out and curls his lip, then he's interested in mating. It means the ewe is in heat."

"Curls his lip? His leg? How do you know these things, baba?"

"My father…his father…probably ten fathers before that. We are Bedouins, Bedu. If you learn the business you can live in the village and not spend your entire life grazing land in faraway places," Wali said as they both watched the ram. "See that? See his lip? She's in heat and they're ready to mate."

"What's mating, grandfather?"

"Noam go get your sticks and your cloth and clean up from our breakfast. You can come back out later," Wali said as he winked at Bedu.

Noam ran off as instructed. Wali and Bedu moved away and left the ram and ewe alone. Atlas rumbled as they came closer.

"How many sheep do you want to buy, Bedu?"

"Seven," he said quickly. "And four goats."

"You can buy goats from everybody else. I only raise Jacob's sheep."

"Then seven sheep, baba."

"Okay, then you breed my entire flock. Care for the ewes and the rams and the horses. I need work done on the fences. I have some projects you can work on in the house as well. Noam needs care every day and someone to play with. In April, you can have half of all newborn lambs. That will be your payment for the work and for Atlas. Then, I'll close your line of credit. Paid in full."

Bedu was overwhelmed. If everything worked well, he may have sixteen or seventeen sheep, far more than what his father was expecting. He suddenly grew sad.

"My parents are expecting me."

Wali nodded his head. "I'm sorry, Bedu. They will be worried. They may even think you're dead."

"Or worse."

"Worse than being dead?" Wali asked.

"What if my father thinks I left him and ran off with the gold coins?"

Wali understood. "That *would* be worse...you're right. I guess that means Abbas will have quite an unexpected celebration next spring when you come home. Well, I'll let you get to work. I need to tend to some of my son's affairs."

"Baba, can we talk tonight? I need to tell you about the promise I made to King Melchior."

"About that girl?"

Bedu nodded.

Several weeks passed. Noam and Bedu played throughout the days, even as Bedu taught the boy how to care for their sheep. Noam would lead the sheep up to the top of the hills behind Wali's farm and guide them to the water on the other side. They played every game imaginable and were always at each other's side. Wali always watched from a distance with a cup of chai in his hand. He seemed pleased, if not relieved.

Bedu suspected that his cousin, Wali, was in fact delighted that Bedu had shown up when he did. The timing was perfect.

"Well, it looks like thirty-two of the ewes are pregnant. Come with me to the merchant's store. We need to buy good hay grasses like orchard and reed canary. The spring rains will give us back the green grass we need. But we'll need to buy legumes in a few months."

"Legumes?" Bedu asked.

"They need the same amounts of legumes as the grass they eat. Nothing fancy, just cowpeas, vetch, soybean...even red clover if we can find it up in the hills."

"I can find it, grandfather."

"Then we have a new job to do," Bedu said to the boy.

"Well, we don't need the red clover yet. You can help Bedu after he gets back."

Bedu was surprised. "Back? Back from where, baba? Where do you need me to go?"

Wali stood up and motioned for Noam and Bedu to follow him to the stables. He pulled the tack room door open and stepped in. Wali pulled the blanket away as dust filled the air.

"A saddle? Baba, I have never ridden a horse before."

"Then it's time to learn. We start today."

"But –."

"It's a long distance from here to Bsharri. But it'll be a much shorter trip on Atlas than on your feet."

Bedu's mouth dropped.

"Bsharri? On Atlas?"

"That's where you said Yasmin was, didn't you? You made a promise, right? So, you shall learn to ride, go check on your king's granddaughter and return in time for the birth of your new business."

"Can I go? Can I go too, grandfather?" Noam pleaded.

"No. You'll wait here with me. You still have chores to do. Looks like you're a shepherd now, Noam."

"How long will it take, baba?" Bedu asked.

Wali thought and calculated the distance in his thoughts. "Well, as long as you don't catch leprosy in Halhul and make it through Efrat alive this time. Don't drown in Jericho, and…you could get to Bsharri in…oh, nine days if Atlas is willing, fifteen if you don't know how to ride very well."

Wali spent the afternoon teaching Bedu how to use a saddle and reins after they returned from seeing the merchant. Atlas already loved Bedu as he had faithfully fed him, walked him and brushed him since he arrived at his cousin's house the month before.

Atlas seemed to be itching to run. It had been far too long since Wali's youngest son had ridden him.

"Okay, step up on the stirrup, get into the saddle, and hold the reins tight. Make sure Atlas senses your confidence or he'll think he's the boss."

Bedu stood up and started to settle into the saddle when Atlas took off like a shooting star. Grazing and pregnant ewes scattered like dust in the wind as Atlas bolted by with Bedu wrapped around his neck for dear life.

Atlas was up and over the nearby hills and gone from sight before Noam and Wali could stop laughing and get up from curled positions in the grass.

"Should we go find them, grandfather?"

Wali couldn't stop laughing. "No, Noam...Atlas will bring him back when he's good and ready."

The sun was nearly down when Wali and Noam saw the silhouette of Atlas and Bedu cresting the top of the hill and heading home.

They were walking.

Slowly.

The grazing ewes hardly even moved out of their way. Atlas walked into the stables. Bedu looked exhausted.

Bedu got down gingerly and removed the saddle and reins from Atlas. The black horse was wet and covered with sweat. Atlas was ready to eat.

"I'll brush you out in the morning, Atlas. Enjoy your grain," Bedu said as he left for the house.

Wali was holding his cup of tea and Noam was smiling by his side. The light from Wali's lantern illuminated the walk and gait of a man who appeared to be old and unsteady. But it was, of course, Bedu who learned first-hand – and the hard way – the adventures of a bored horse who was ready to run.

"Hungry?" Wali said as Noam hid his laughter in his grand-father's robe.

Bedu said nothing but smiled as he hobbled into the house, his legs still gaping in the now rigid shape of Atlas once beneath him.

The January morning had finally arrived. The air was crisp and cool. The days were much shorter. Noam ran to Bedu and hugged him.

"I want to go with you, Bedu."

"Not this time, okay?"

"Will you come back? Or are you going to leave me like my baba did?" Noam began to cry. "I love you, Bedu…please come back."

Bedu held the boy close. He had never heard someone other than his mother and father say that they loved him. Certainly not his little sister, Amira. Wali was touched and wiped away a tear or two. Bedu was most definitely part of his family now, almost like a son.

"Here, I want you to wear these." Wali handed Bedu his son's riding clothes. Bedu immediately thought of Javad. Even a black scarf for his forehead. "If you're going to ride Atlas that fast, you best look more like a rider than a chicken hanging on to an Arabian horse."

Noam laughed.

Bedu changed clothes. When he returned, Wali handed him his satchel. "There are some shekels of silver in there, in case you need it."

"But baba," Bedu started before Wali could hush him.

"Consider it an advance on your payment. Go check on your woman and then get back here quickly. The ewes will need legumes in a month."

"Thank you, baba…but she's not '*my woman*.'"

"Looking the way that you do, riding up on Atlas, with all of the stories you have to tell…she will be, my son, she will be," Wali said with a wink.

"I'm just a shepherd boy from Damascus, baba."

"That's what you *did* but that's not who you *are*, Bedu. Now you are becoming someone new…maybe even better."

Atlas must have figured that nine days was a slow saunter, so he delivered Bedu to Bsharri in eight.

Bsharri was much colder than Bedu had imagined. He could see snow on the ground in the mountains. The wind was blowing hard.

He stopped at the first store he saw and asked about the young Persian woman. Of course, everyone in Bsharri knew about the army that arrived and built her the most beautiful house in the District.

"You mean the tree woman," the man in the store said confidently.

"Tree woman?" Bedu asked.

"Yes, she says she's here to study the cedars and plant more offspring from their shoots. Seedlings she called them."

"Yes, *that's* the woman."

"Up in the mountains. Only one road leading up there. You can't miss her house. Never seen anything like it before. She's there, unless she's already frozen to death. She doesn't even have a husband. Did you know that?"

Bedu nodded and thanked the man for his time. Atlas had him to her house in only a few minutes.

Bedu tied Atlas to a tree. It was already dark. The stars bounced off the snow and he could see trees the size of which he could not fathom. But her house was something he had never seen before either.

It was completely made of wood.

Lanterns burned brightly outside and lit the yellowish tint of the wood. As he walked up the stone-laid path, he came face-to-face with an enormous door made of wood. It was fixed in place with large iron hinges that anchored the door into the beams on one side. It was more than he could imagine.

The windows were shuttered tightly with more wood, but he noticed flickering light inside and between the slats. The chimney made of large stones poured billows of smoke from the top of the roof that was angled. There was a horseshoe attached to the front door. It moved front and back, in and out with a creaking sound. He reached for it and then let go. It made a knock. He pulled it back again, then again.

He heard footsteps approaching on the other side of the door.

"Who's there?" he heard the woman's voice say.

"It is me, Bedu, the shepherd boy from Damascus. Your grandfather asked me to come and check on you."

There was silence.

"I'm fine. Thank you for checking," she finally said.

Bedu dropped his head. He was slightly disappointed to say the least. But he had fulfilled his promise. He was sure of that. He walked over to Atlas and untied the reins from the small tree that was dwarfed by the others. He heard a shutter clasp loosen and noticed a shutter push open ever so slightly by the window on the side of the house.

"You are the poet?" Yasmin asked as Bedu pulled Atlas around.

"I am. And now I hear that you are the tree woman," Bedu said as he mounted Atlas.

"That's your horse?"

"It is. I'm glad you are well. Tell your grandfather that I fulfilled my promise."

"Wait. You're leaving?"

"I wasn't invited to stay. Good night."

Bedu and Atlas ran down the road off the mountain and back into Bsharri. It was too cold to sleep outside, so he found the inn.

"How much for a room? Just one night," Bedu asked.

"One shekel of silver," the man said. "You can board your horse in the stables behind the inn."

Bedu opened his satchel for the first time since he had left Hebron. The hidden pocket was filled with silver coins. He handed one to the innkeeper.

Atlas was fed and bedded down for the night. A stable boy took Atlas and offered him some grain.

"Is this your father's inn?"

The boy nodded. "I handle his stables at night and tend to our sheep during the day."

"So, you're a shepherd?" Bedu asked.

The boy hesitated.

"I am now…but I want to write poems and be a teacher when I'm older."

"Poems? Do you go to school?" Bedu asked.

"No. I'm trying to help my father and mother. Besides, there are no schools nearby for the children of Bsharri. So, my mother teaches me what she knows."

Bedu understood. It was the same for him when he was a younger boy.

"My name is Bedu, I'm a shepherd boy from Damascus."

"With this horse? I think you are really a king. My name is Tamir."

"Thank you, Tamir. Watch over Atlas and make sure he's comfortable tonight. We have a long journey in the morning.

Bedu headed to his room to sleep. It would be a long, if not disappointing, ride back to Wali and Noam.

With morning light, Bedu left the inn and walked back to the stables. He saw the boy brushing out Atlas.

"Well, that was very nice of -." Bedu stopped in his steps as Tamir turned around. "Yasmin?"

"You frightened me last night. I couldn't be sure it was really you."

"I'm sorry."

"He's yours?" she said as she rubbed Atlas.

"Yes. I've been down in Hebron. I bought him there. He once belonged to my cousin who died with the fever."

Yasmin continued to brush. "So, Tamir told me you're leaving today."

"That is my plan."

"Well, there's a room in my stables and a hot fire in my fireplace. Would you like to eat before you leave? Perhaps stay a night or two?"

Bedu could already feel the warmth of her fireplace even while standing in the middle of a cold stable behind the Bsharri inn.

"I would like that very much."

Yasmin reached over and pulled the saddle off the post and threw it over the back of Atlas. With three quick moves, pulls and snaps, he was ready to go. Atlas seemed to appreciate the speed for a change.

Yasmin climbed up into the saddle then slipped off the backside to the bare hide of the Arabian.

"Come on…you don't expect me to walk up the mountain, do you? I've already walked down it this morning in the cold darkness."

Bedu put his foot in the stirrup and climbed up. Yasmin wrapped her arms around him.

"How did you know that I would be here?" Bedu asked as he led Atlas out and onto the road.

"There's no place else in Bsharri. It wasn't hard to find you."

The inside of Yasmin's house was like nothing he had ever seen before. There was no dirt on the floor. It was made of long wood planks. There was furniture. Tables. Benches. Even chairs with fabric.

She brought him a plate of eggs, fruit and cheese as he sat among the pillows around the warm fire and the crackling hearth.

"Grandfather gave you five gold coins, to replace your father's livestock. Did you do that?"

Bedu closed his eyes. He couldn't bear the thought of telling her that he had stolen five more from King Melchior. "She must never know what terrible thing I have done," he persuaded himself.

"I'm still working on that," Bedu finally said.

"But it's January. What have you been doing and why have you waited so long?"

For the next few hours, Bedu told her about the boy in the floods near Jericho, the misfortune he endured on the road to Efrat, the stone fence he rebuilt, the three shekels of silver and the new satchel the kind woman made for him. He told her about the outcasts near Halhul, the twenty kabobs and then Hebron. He told her all about Wali and especially Noam. He even told her how he knew when ewes were in heat.

Every word Bedu spoke must have sounded like poetry to Yasmin's ears. She was enamored with his adventure.

"Your words...the way you tell stories...you truly are a poet, Bedu."

Bedu laughed. "Well, Tamir – the stable boy – said that only a king could ride Atlas."

"Then that makes you a poet king, Bedu. A poet king."

"Enough about my story. Why do they call you the tree woman, Yasmin? Because your house is made of wood?"

"No. I would never cut down one of these magnificent cedars. This is the forest of God. But those who came before just took the massive trunks for their works and left the mountain scattered with branches and limbs that are hundreds of years old as well. It is a cruel reminder – a cemetery littered with majesty – of where the mighty cedars once stood. My grandfather's army gathered it all up, cleaned the mountain, and gave all that was discarded and rejected, a new life. Now I call it home."

"So, why the tree woman?" Bedu pressed.

"The Phoenicians, Romans, Greeks, Persians, Israelites, Egyptians – just about any kingdom you can name – have all come to these forests to take the trees for their strong wood. They leave nothing but scars. They build great ships, great temples, great whatever – and they leave rubble and debris in their footsteps. If everyone does this, how long before the forest of God is gone? Gone forever."

"This is why you moved here? To take care of trees?" Bedu asked. There was something magical, mystical, almost noble, about her love for the cedars.

"My father – even more so my grandfather – have both always told me that life has no limits if you have values and morals and healthy desires. Grandfather wanted me out of Persia."

"Why?"

"In Persia, I am a woman living in an old culture with new expectations as to who I am, what my role is to be, and what is expected of me. Here, I am just a person. The 'tree woman' who lives in a house on the mountain surrounded by the forest of God."

"And snow," Bedu added.

"And snow."

"Yasmin, I understand that you love the trees, but what can you do to save them from becoming beams on ships or posts in a temple? I mean, you're just one person," Bedu asked with genuine interest.

"Do you want to learn?" Yasmin said excitedly as she sprang to her feet. "Come on." Yasmin ran out of the room and grabbed a coat, as Bedu followed her outside to the stables where Atlas was enjoying his oats. She opened the door in the back of the open stables and entered a closed room. A room with plenty of room to sleep, Bedu noted.

"While my father's soldiers were building my house, I hiked through the forest, day after day, collecting the cones that had already fallen from the trees. I wrapped them in cloth in darkness so they could fully ripen. Once ripe, the scales on the cone begin to crack open. Early in December, the scales started to drop their seeds."

"You're going to plant trees?"

Yasmin was full of energy and life. She walked him over to ten wooden pails against the outside wall. "Each pail was filled with water and I poured seeds into all ten pails of water, but only for a few hours. The seeds that floated, were no good and had to be thrown out. The seeds that sunk, they were alive and ready to grow."

"How do you know all of this? Who taught you?"

"The seeds have been wrapped in wet cheesecloth for a month now. I keep them in here," Yasmin said as she opened a hidden cupboard that was neither in the stable room for warmth, nor outside in the cold. "I misted the seeds every day. Can't let them dry out."

"You're going to plant seeds...on the mountain...for the rest of your life?"

"Today is an exciting day for me, Bedu. Come here." Yasmin pulled a large tarp off the pile in the back of the room beneath the shuttered window. "For the last few months, I have been making these small wooden pots from the discarded wood all over the forest floor. See the hole in the bottom? It's there so the water can drip out and not drown the seeds."

"You made all of these pots?" Bedu asked astonished.

"Each morning I go out with two pails. One, I scoop up sand from the higher elevations and in the other I carefully pull peat moss out and the black dirt around it."

"What's special about today?"

"Today, you and I are going to plant one hundred seeds."

"Isn't it too cold to plant seeds now? We never plant our vegetables until the spring."

"Not in the ground…in these pots. We need to fill each one of the pots with sand and peat, cover each seed in grandfather's powder, cover the seeds below the mixture, then add some water."

"Grandfather's powder…King Melchior has special powders, too?"

Yasmin laughed. "He's not a king. But he is a wise man. He knows everything, I think. He gave me this powder. He said if I coat the seeds in the powder, blow off the extra, it will protect the seeds from fungus."

"That's it? From these little pots you'll have these huge trees?"

"Not quite that easy. I have a shelter built in the front of the house, facing the southern sky. The seeds need six to eight hours of sunlight each day. In about a month – maybe March – the seeds will start to germinate with little cedar sprouts. That gives me about six weeks to make one hundred more pails, larger this time, so the seeds have room to grow. While they're in the larger pails, I'll go out onto the mountain and find one hundred places to build beds where they'll grow and spend the rest of their lives."

"I have never seen a tree like these, Yasmin. Have you measured any of them?"

"We'll do that next. They can live one to two thousand years, Bedu. Imagine, two thousand years from now – 2030 – what we plant today might still be alive then. Each tree will tell many stories, but they will always be my babies. That's why I'm the tree woman. Doing something I love, beyond myself, that's who I am."

Bedu was filled with a million thoughts. Sheep come and go. Some are for wool. Some are for milk, or cheese or meat. But none are for a thousand years, let alone two.

"Let's go," Yasmin said as she raced out the door, past Atlas and up the side of the mountain.

"Where are we going?" Bedu yelled form behind.

"You'll see."

Yasmin climbed up a steep trail to a plateau. She stood proudly beneath the largest tree, perhaps the largest – and oldest – tree in the world. Bedu stood in silent awe. The singular trunk was thicker and wider than most fishing boats he had seen on the Galilee. The height was indescribable, and the branches grew out horizontally and spiraled to the top.

"Come help me," Yasmin said as she ran up to the tree and spread her arms out as wide as she could, from left to right. "My right fingers are in this rut. Let's measure all the way around until we get back to the rut."

"Okay…" Bedu said, completely unsure of the plan.

"Put your right fingers on my left hand and spread out and around the tree." Bedu did as instructed, though he felt uncomfortable touching her hand. But before he could question, she pulled away and moved to his left. "Don't move." Her right fingers were now on his left hand. She was touching him and that was not uncomfortable at all. "Go," she said not the least bit concerned about touching hands. Bedu ran behind her and they both moved until they were back at the rut.

"How big?" Bedu asked, expecting a scientific measurement.

"Five Yasmin's and four-and-a-half Bedu's." They both fell to the snow laughing. Yasmin scooped up a handful and threw it in Bedu's face as she ran down the mountain laughing.

Bedu had never felt anything before like what he was feeling now. "I'm a shepherd boy from Damascus," he thought, "and I'm chasing a princess down her mountain throwing snowballs."

The house was filled with the aromas of vegetables and spices like he had never smelled before. And Yasmin had something that he had never eaten at before and he liked it.

A table.

Though young, she was a proper lady. She enjoyed fine linens and fancy dishes. Everything in her home was perfect. Clearly, she had never lived as a Bedouin before, Bedu concluded.

Bedu was exhausted. They spent the whole afternoon potting, coating, planting and watering one hundred seeds. As happy as he was, Bedu had mixed emotions. Even if Yasmin was being kind to him, how could she ever leave *this* to be the wife of a Bedouin shepherd boy? They were just too different.

But he was hungry. They were both hungry.

"Can you stir the vegetables and put some rice on our plates?" she asked as she pulled a pot off the fire.

Bedu was surprised. He had seen Wali cook and work in the kitchen to feed Noam but that was because his wife was dead. Abbas never worked in the kitchen with Yara. That was Amira's job.

Bedu jumped up. He didn't hesitate. He stirred the vegetables with a wooden spoon then grabbed the iron handles on the rice pot.

"Ouch. They're blazing hot," Bedu exclaimed as he fanned his hands in the air.

"Use the cloth, silly," Yasmin laughed.

Everything about the day and the meal was perfect. The fire in the hearth crackled and warmed their souls as much as the vegetables, spices and rice warmed their bodies.

"Well, I suppose I should get down to the inn before it gets too late."

"Nonsense. You can stay in the stable room. There's a small firepit out there and I have extra blankets. Besides, Atlas will enjoy your company."

"That's okay? I mean, you're not married."

"You're not married either, are you?"

"No."

"Then don't worry about someone else's rules. I think we'll be just fine." Bedu nodded.

"I will leave tomorrow, Yasmin, I need to get back to Hebron. I have much work to do with the pregnant ewes as we move them over to a different diet."

Yasmin fell silent.

She got up from the table and walked over to the fireplace and sat on the floor, staring into the flames.

"When will you be back?" she finally asked.

Bedu was shocked. His visit had already fulfilled the promise he had made to King Melchior. He didn't even contemplate a day he would ever come back.

"Soon," Bedu said with a sound he never knew was going to escape his lips. "Unless you rent the stable room out to somebody else."

She smiled. "I'll be expecting you then. You must stay longer. Perhaps for the summer? I'll plant the seedlings into the larger pots that I will build. Then maybe you and Atlas can help me get them up the mountain to their beds?"

Bedu could see it all. It would be wonderful.

"Then, each year, the cedar will grow the length of my elbow to my fingers," Yasmin continued. "And after forty years...*forty* years... it, too, will produce seeds for another generation of cedars in the forest of God. I will plant them, too."

Bedu thought about forty years. He was only twenty-one and he heard Yasmin tell Amira that she was nineteen.

"Combined together, we are only forty years. Will you be here to see that generation of seeds, Yasmin?"

"I pray. My grandfather is only ninety-two and he will probably live forever, it seems. But my mother died in childbirth. It is not ours to know when we die, but I pray."

The next morning, after a warm breakfast and an awkward goodbye outside Yasmin's front door with iron hinges, Atlas and Bedu headed down the mountain for the long ride back to Hebron.

He had fulfilled his promise to King Melchior, but it did not free him of the guilt of five gold coins.

Bedu stopped at the inn and left his horse with Tamir and went inside.

"We have no rooms to rent this early in the morning," the innkeeper yelled from behind the counter, not even bothering to look at his customer.

"I'm not here for a room. I want to hire your son, Tamir."

The man looked up from the counter.

"Tamir? For what?"

"I need a shepherd boy who will deliver seven sheep and four goats to my home in Damascus and give my family a message."

"Damascus? The boy is only twelve."

"I did it. He can do it. It's nine days walking there with the animals. Eight days back. Tamir said you had a flock."

"A small one."

"Can you sell me seven sheep and four goats?"

"Maybe."

"Do you have Jacob's sheep?"

"No. They cost too much money."

"Because they're the best. Where can I buy Jacob's sheep?"

The innkeeper paused. "My cousin has them. I could have Tamir buy from him, but for a profit of course."

"How much?"

The innkeeper thought for a while. The man did pay for a room the night before. Tamir had told him that he had a beautiful black Arabian.

"Thirty shekels of silver."

Bedu acted like he was shocked by the price.

"And for Tamir?"

"Included. He does what I tell him to do."

Bedu reached into his satchel and pulled out thirty shekels of silver and laid them on the innkeeper's counter. The man was clearly surprised that Bedu accepted his price and that so much silver was sitting in front of him.

"I will make the arrangements with Tamir," Bedu said as he walked out the door and back to the stables.

"You're leaving already, king?" Tamir asked as Bedu walked up.

"I'm not a king, Tamir. I made arrangements with your father. I'm hiring you as a shepherd boy to take seven Jacob's sheep and four goats to my father's house in Damascus. His name is Abbas. You must tell them that I am fine and will be at Wali's house in Hebron for a long time."

"You paid my father?"

"Thirty shekels of silver. But I have something for you, too."

The boy seemed puzzled.

"You said you had many friends but there is no school here for you."

"Yes."

Bedu reached into his satchel and pulled out all the remaining silver coins from the hidden pocket inside his sheepskin satchel.

Tamir's eyes lit up. Bedu counted each one as he dropped them into Tamir's hands.

"Eight…and nine. Your father will pay you for your journey to Damascus and back."

"Then what's *this* for?"

"I will be back in a few months. Gather up all your friends that want to learn, that want to go to school. I'm going to start a school, Tamir."

"Here in Bsharri?" the boy said with unbridled excitement.

"Right here."

"What will we learn?"

"Well…how to breed sheep and grow cedar trees to start with. Then? Poetry. Writing. Reading. How to speak and tell stories."

"This is a dream. I love you king. I have always wished for this. I will have at least ten friends ready for school when you return."

Bedu touched the boy's head gently, mounted Atlas, and started the ride back to Hebron with an empty satchel and a heart full of joy.

Bedu and Atlas camped in the hills of Chtoura the first night. He unfolded his bedroll and laid down.

Stars filled the heavens like he had never seen before. Bedu realized that not all stars were white or the same color. Some seemed yellow, some were orange, some were even blue. But one star seemed brighter than all the others. In fact, it was close to the first two stars he had already noticed before.

Bedu leaned back and took it all in. It was what six other men did for the mother of a drowning son. It was the unequivocal determination that a stranger and his wife felt after he was robbed in

Efrat. The outcast mother had the same thing for her hungry children. It was how Wali built a business for himself and his sons and now Bedu was doing the same thing for Noam, guiding him to care for sheep. It was evident in Tamir's excitement over a school and his willingness to recruit students. And it was Yasmin's vision for the cedars of God.

It was leadership; conceived in love for others and nurtured by the dedication to achieve something greater.

L eadership: *When leaders love beyond self, life replaces emptiness and indecision with fulfillment and purpose.*

5

NOAM MUST HAVE HEARD ATLAS COMING THROUGH TOWN AS HE RAN FULL SPEED DOWN THE ROAD, THEN LEFT PAST TWO STREETS AND INTO THE MIDDLE OF HEBRON AS BEDU RETURNED.

Bedu jumped off the horse with as much excitement as Noam had for him. They embraced in the middle of the road, in front of the merchant's store.

"I missed you so much, baba. Thank you for coming home."

Bedu was stunned. No one had ever called him 'baba' before.

"I missed you, too, Noam. How is your grandfather?"

"Not well, baba. My uncles say he has the fever, too."

Bedu was filled with sadness, but his face never showed concern to Noam.

"I don't think so, Noam. He's probably just tired. He needs us to do his chores, to tend to his flock so he can rest. That's probably all," Bedu said not even believing his own words.

Noam climbed up into the saddle and Bedu walked them both back to the house. Wali was not at the door to greet them.

Atlas was pleased to be back in the stalls with Athena, a beautiful Arabian mare named for the Greek goddess of wisdom, poetry, and art. Even though she wasn't the real daughter of Zeus, Bedu didn't think Atlas seemed to mind.

Bedu and Noam walked into the house. Wali waved from his bedroll on the floor, a cold, wet cloth on his forehead.

"I told you," Wali struggled to Noam. "I told you he would come back."

"Yes, you did, grandfather, yes you did."

"Are you ill, baba? Noam said your other sons have come to see you."

Wali waved his hand to stop the conversation. "Why don't you two go check on the sheep. We can talk tonight after Noam goes to sleep."

Noam was fast asleep after several hours of playing with two sticks and a cloth while chasing Bedu around the pond in the upper pasture after checking on the pregnant ewes.

Wali motioned him to come closer so they could speak quietly.

"Can I get you more soup, baba?" Wali shook his head.

"Have *you* been feeling well, Bedu?" Wali asked with great concern.

"Me? I have never felt better. I'm feeling things I have never felt before. My life is magical, baba. Yes, I am very well."

Wali smiled.

"I wasn't asking about the girl…but I'm glad it went well."

Bedu blushed.

"Some get the fever…some do not. Noam seems fine. I was afraid that maybe you would not fare well."

"I'm fine, baba. I'm fine."

"I tried to take care of my son and his wife, Bedu. And that's probably where I caught it."

"What, baba?"

"The fever."

"No, baba. You're just tired. I'm here now and I will take care of you and all the sheep and even Noam. I love you like my own father, baba."

"And Noam?" Wali asked. "Do you love him like your own son?"

Tears streamed down Bedu's cheeks. "More than you'll ever know, baba. He brings me so much life and laughter. I wish he really was my son."

Wali pushed himself up to his elbows then started to cough. Bedu helped him sit up and then put a pillow behind his back.

"I'm dying, Bedu. If my journey is like my son's, I have two or three months. Maybe less."

"Baba, please don't talk that way."

"I have already spoken with my three other sons. They agree."

"Agree with what, baba?"

"If you will promise to take Noam, to keep him, love him, and teach him like he was your own…then Noam should be your son."

"Baba…" Bedu tried to speak through his tears but couldn't.

"If you will raise Noam as your son, then I will give you my youngest son's portion of the inheritance. You can have all my animals in addition to the lambs that will rightfully belong to you. I will close out your line of credit. You and my sons can decide what to do with this house and the land."

"Baba, no…" Bedu pleaded.

Wali motioned to the back wall. "See that box, Bedu?"

Bedu nodded.

"When I die, that box belongs to you and Noam. You may not open it until then."

Bedu worked hard in the fields with the ewes. He bought cowpeas, vetch, and soybean from the merchants as Noam gathered red clover in the hills above the pond. Wali wasn't pleased, but Bedu even taught Noam how to ride Athena. She was gentler than Atlas and instinctively seemed to know she was carrying precious cargo.

By the middle of April, almost all the ewes had borne their lambs. The flock had risen to almost seventy. All were Jacob's sheep, the finest in the land.

Wali had not eaten in two days. He was still asleep. Bedu laid his head on Wali's chest.

Nothing.

Bedu and Noam held each other, weeping, then laughing as they told stories about Wali, then weeping some more. Noam got up and grabbed the black scarf that was in his grandfather's drawer. Together, he and Bedu wrapped it around the post by the front door.

The three brothers arrived for the funeral, but they would not come into Wali's house. They kept their distance from Bedu and Noam, too.

Nobody really understood the fever or who it might attack next.

The brothers were gathered on the other side of Wali's stone and mud wall. Bedu and Noam walked out to greet them.

"Bedu?" the oldest asked as Bedu nodded. "I am Binyamin, Wali's oldest son."

"I have heard about you, Binyamin. Your father was proud of you, proud of all your brothers."

Binyamin covered his heart.

"You will take Noam, then?"

"As my son."

Binyamin nodded. "My father has given you all of his animals, as well as Atlas and Athena for your work and now your care. He also has a box for you. It's your portion of our brother's inheritance and is to be used for Noam's care."

"I understand," Bedu said. Noam wrapped his arms around his baba.

"Do you wish to keep our father's house?"

Bedu didn't know what to say. Perhaps they expected him to stay and raise Noam in Hebron.

"No, Uncle Binyamin," Noam shouted. "We are going to Bsharri, to live in the forest of God. Baba Bedu is opening a school there."

Bedu was shocked, but not so much that he couldn't smile.

"You're a teacher?" Binyamin asked. "I thought you were just a shepherd boy from Damascus."

Bedu took a few steps forward as Binyamin and his brothers took equal steps back and away from him.

"That's what I once *did*...but that's not who I want to *be*."

"Okay, then we will sell the house and his land. We have our own homes and businesses and none of our wives are willing to come here anymore…not after this."

That night, Noam was asleep when Bedu poured another cup of chai. His eyes caught the unopened box every few seconds. He couldn't move. He dared not touch it, even though he knew it was his and his alone.

Bedu fell asleep. He dreamed of many things, but one thing was startling. His father, Abbas, was handing him the box. "Open it. Open the box, Bedu. It's yours."

Bedu awoke and sat up quickly. Noam was still sleeping soundly next to him. He got up and moved to the box. He picked it up. It was heavier than he thought it would be. He shook it slightly until Noam stirred. Bedu took the box into the kitchen and lit the oil lamp.

He lifted the lid slowly, carefully, until it was all the way open. Bedu's eyes grew larger than the cups for chai.

The box was filled with gold coins, sixty of them that Bedu counted, maybe more. It was a lifetime of work, a successful business, and the youngest son's share of great fortune. Bedu realized he could never spend that much money, not in his entire lifetime.

But he did have some ideas.

Nothing was more important than the journey that would start in the morning. He and Noam would lead a herd of sixty-eight sheep and six rams with Athena and Atlas all the way to Bsharri and the forest of God.

It would be a very long adventure. He hoped to be back in time to help Yasmin plant her one hundred cedar seedlings on the mountain.

For the next six days they traveled through Efrat, Jerusalem, Nablus, Afula, Nazareth and finally on the northwestern shore of the Sea of Galilee, between Capernaum and Gennesarat. There was plenty of water and green grass. They decided to rest the sheep for a day before the final push north to Bsharri.

Bedu and Noam finished their breakfast around the fire. Atlas and Athena were grazing in the shade of trees as the sheep huddled nearby and the rams behaved themselves.

Noam stood up and pointed.

"Look, baba…many people are coming."

Bedu looked. Noam was right. Not just many people but hundreds of people, a multitude.

"Are we in danger?" Noam asked with a hint of fear in his voice.

"I don't think so, Noam. They seem to be sitting. Maybe it's a festival or a large wedding party."

"Out here?"

Bedu shook his head. "I don't know."

Suddenly, a man climbed up on the rock ledge overlooking the valley where the people sat and where Bedu and Noam camped with their herd and horses down below.

He began to speak. His voice echoed off the rock walls of the hills and bounced back from the water of Galilee.

"Blessed are the poor in spirit," The Speaker began. The people were mesmerized.

"Blessed are the meek, for they shall be comforted…blessed are they that mourn, for they shall be comforted…blessed are they that hunger and thirst after justice for they shall have their fill."

"What is he saying, baba?" Noam asked.

"Poetry…it's beautiful poetry…words like I have never heard before."

"Who is he? A teacher?"

"I don't know, Noam. He's The Speaker, I guess."

"Blessed are the merciful for they shall obtain it…blessed are the clean of heart."

"His words are so simple and yet so profound," Bedu whispered.

"Blessed are the peacemakers for they shall be called children of God…"

The Speaker went on for several minutes. The crowd did not stir. Bedu and Noam did not move. The sheep were quiet, even the horses seemed to be listening as well. Then he heard it. In a split second, Bedu's life was changed.

"Treat others the way you wish they would treat you."

"What does that mean, baba? What The Speaker just said. What does it mean?"

Bedu paused and reflected.

"They are 'be' attitudes…he's telling us that who we are on the inside, guides our words, thoughts and actions on the outside. It means…if you treat a stranger like a friend, then he will treat you like his friend. If you are honest in your dealings, others will be honest with you. If you give love and laughter, others will give you the same. If you…give an outcast food, then someday – when you're hungry – someone will give you food, too. When you are willing to save someone else's life, someday someone will try to save yours. If you treat someone like they are a king…then they will treat you like a king."

Noam was silent. The words from The Speaker touched his heart as they touched Bedu.

"It means...if you steal five gold coins from one, then some-one will steal them from you," Bedu said as both guilt and a new awareness filled his spirit. "It all makes sense, Noam. I understand. It's like a lantern has been lit in my heart."

Noam looked up at Bedu, his new baba. He was more than a little bit concerned.

"Is the lantern hot? Do you think you have the fever, too, baba?"

Bedu laughed and rolled Noam over in the grass and tick-led him so that his laughter echoed off the same rocks as The Speaker's words.

The crowds were gone, and night filled the sky. Bedu and Noam laid back on their bedrolls and admired the heavens.

"See that star, baba? The bright one right there," Noam said pointing. "What does it mean?"

Bedu smiled. "It means treat people well, and they'll treat you well in return."

Treat: *Treat people – all people – well, no matter their station or position in life, and they will treat you well.*

6

ATHENA AND ATLAS LED THE WAY UP THE WIND-
ING ROAD TO THE MIDDLE OF THE MOUNTAIN IN
THE FOREST OF GOD. Sixty-eight sheep and six rams
followed faithfully behind.

Yasmin's house came into view but there was no smoke in the
chimney and the snow was gone.

Bedu and Noam walked up to the solid wood door that was
hanging on iron hinges. Bedu pulled the horseshoe back three times.
Noam looked on with astonishment.

Yasmin didn't speak through the door this time. She opened it
with a huge smile for Bedu, then looked down at Noam, and finally
focused on more than seventy animals standing in her front yard.

"Bedu?" she asked gingerly.

"Yasmin. I've missed you. This is Noam, my son. Remember, I
told you about him?" Bedu said proudly as Yasmin looked stunned.

"Son?"

Bedu turned and eagerly pointed to his enormous herd. "Well,
what do you think?"

"Why are they all in my front yard, Bedu?"

Noam couldn't hold back the giggles.

"Well, we just got here from Hebron and I thought we would just -."

"You obviously *didn't* think. Please get them off my yard. Now!" With that, Yasmin shut her door with a little more swing than what normally might be required to close a solid cedar door hung on iron hinges.

"That went well," Noam said as he held back the laughter. "I thought you said you two were -." Bedu hushed him before he could finish his words.

"Let's head back down the road to Bsharri. We need to find a boy named Tamir."

The innkeeper was pleased to see Bedu again, though somewhat surprised that he brought his son along this time. Bedu paid the shekel of silver for the room before he and Noam took the flock behind the inn and into the open corral. Atlas and Athena were ready for oats.

Tamir was happy to see Bedu as well.

"King Bedu," Tamir yelled. "I delivered the seven sheep and four goats to your father, Abbas. Your mother cried for an hour when I told her you were alive and living in Hebron."

"You're a king?" Noam whispered.

"I'm not a king. Tamir, thank you very much. You did good work. And my sister, Amira?"

"Yes, king…she is well…and very cute."

"My sister?"

"Are all of these sheep yours?" Tamir asked.

"All of them, and the rams, and the horses," Noam chimed in with great pride.

"Then you are a wealthy king. Oh, and we are all ready," Tamir said as he poured oats into Athena's feeder.

"Ready for what?" Bedu asked.

"The school. I have more than forty boys who say they are ready to learn and go to school."

Noam was surprised.

"That's great," Bedu answered. "How many girls?"

"My father says that girls don't go to school. Only mothers teach the girls."

Bedu pulled the saddle off Atlas and put it on the post as Atlas got a fresh pour of oats as well.

"Not in my school, Tamir. Girls go to my school, too."

"But king?"

"No girls… no school, Tamir. Simple as that."

"Speak to my father when you go back in. He owns an empty house on the other side of Bsharri District that is open. It has a large field and stables. It belonged to my grandfather. Maybe it could be your school."

After a brief conversation with the innkeeper in the morning, Bedu paid for another night's stay and they saddled-up Athena and Atlas to go look at the empty house that belonged to Tamir's late grandfather.

Bedu and Noam walked through the house, through the back fields and over to the stables.

"It's nice," said Noam.

"Not as nice as baba Wali's house but nicer – and much larger – than my home in Damascus," Bedu added.

"I could live here," Noam concluded with a smile beaming ear to ear.

"Me too. Me too." Bedu's words faded and he looked off in the distance toward the mountain.

"But…?" Noam prodded.

"My father is getting older…my mother…maybe we should return home and help them, take over his farm. That's what Bedouins do."

"But you have five times the herd of your baba…you have horses. You said their house is smaller. And what about Yasmin? You like her, don't you?"

Bedu kicked at the dirt. "You saw her face. She would never marry a shepherd boy from Damascus."

"Is that who you are, baba? I just heard Tamir say you were a teacher and that you would have a school. My grandfather taught you how to make a business. You inherited my father's share of baba Wali's gift. And you think you're still a shepherd boy from Damascus? Have you opened your eyes yet, baba? Why can't you see?"

Bedu was filled with an instant energy and determination unlike anything he had ever felt before. His thoughts flashed like lightning in his mind.

"You are right, son. Let's build a school. We can move my father and mother here if they wish. We can care for them and live as one large family."

Bedu negotiated with the innkeeper and bought the house, the land and the stables for ten shekels of gold. He and Noam stopped by the yard where men were building fishing boats and Bedu bought four canvas sewn sails. He hired those men to bury six large posts in the ground next to the stables and they stretched the canvas sails across the tops of the posts to provide shelter from the sun and rain to the outdoor classroom below.

Tamir and Noam got the classroom ready as Bedu went into town and recruited a widow who knew how to read, write and teach Aramaic. Her brothers agreed to let her work.

Bedu decided the children would have four classes every day. The first would be language. They would learn to read and write every morning for two hours. The next class would be animal care and breeding. Bedu would teach that himself. In the afternoon, the innkeeper would teach math so that each child could learn some common-sense principles about basic money.

The fourth class would have to wait.

The first day of school came quickly. Tamir marched seven boys down the middle of Bsharri District and into the new canvas school by the stables.

"I thought you said forty boys, Tamir?" Bedu whispered as the boys sat down.

"This is forty, king," Tamir answered.

"Make sure you really pay attention in your math class this afternoon, Tamir. Okay?"

Bedu was going to dismiss the seven boys, plus Tamir and Noam, after the third class, the math class taught by the innkeeper. But the students protested.

"What about the fourth class?" asked one.

Bedu stammered. "We're not ready for that one yet. It has to do with trees."

"Well, I'm not leaving until I've had a fourth class. My mama thinks I'm taking four classes," said one.

"Me neither," said another.

"What about a poetry class, baba?" Noam whispered.

Bedu searched for his thoughts then moved to the front of the classroom.

"Anyone can say words. We all know words. But when your words can paint a picture that others can see, hear, and feel while you're talking...well, that's poetry. Like this: 'I was once a young boy...a shepherd...a shepherd boy from Damascus. Every night, just about the same time, *she* would come speak to me as I lay by the pond in the green, green grasses of a field...she was like no other... she had captured my heart and my imagination... she filled my mind with thoughts and my heart with dreams...she moved toward me slowly at first, then faster...each night she reached out and kissed my eyes with gold and pink hues...she whispered through flames of red and orange as they danced across the sky...she was mine... only mine...yes, she spoke to all shepherd boys on different hills... if...if they were patient and waited for her each night. Goodnight my love...goodnight...tell your stories to all other shepherd boys while I sleep but come back to me in the morning...on the other side of the hills...and tell me new stories with gold, and pink, reds and orange.'"

The boys were silent. They had never heard such beautiful words.

"Well?" Bedu finally asked.

"A sunset? You told us about a sunset, didn't you?" Tamir asked.

Bedu nodded his head.

"That's poetry. When you take things that you see and experience every day and put them into words that make them feel alive and fresh and new for the first time, that's poetry."

The boys stood up for the march back home.

"Can we have the poetry class until you're ready for the tree class?" one boy asked.

"Okay, we can do that. But we need girls, Tamir. Find some girls."

The next morning, the class grew to eleven and by the end of the second week, twenty-one boys were attending. Bedu was excited. Noam had more friends than he ever had before in his life.

But still, there were no girls.

There was no school on Saturday. Noam got up early and finished his morning chores well before Bedu even had his first cup of tea. Athena was saddled and tied off by the front door of their new house as Bedu walked outside.

"Noam? Are you going somewhere?"

"I want to go play with Tamir, baba. I finished all of my chores."

"You need to take Athena? Can't you just walk to the inn?"

"Tamir wants to go riding with me, baba. Please?"

Bedu smiled. He guessed this is what it meant to be a father. He wanted Noam to have fun, but he wanted to protect him and keep him safe as well.

"Okay, but not too far. No galloping. I want you home by lunch," Bedu said as Noam *galloped* away into Bsharri District.

TAMIR WAS WAITING as planned and his horse was saddled. They took the shortcut and then up the road to the mountain where the forest of God was growing and the "tree woman" lived.

Noam was too short so Tamir pulled the horseshoe back three times on the wooden door that hung on iron hinges.

Yasmin opened the door. She saw Noam and his friend then looked around. Bedu was nowhere in sight.

"Noam? Did you two come alone?" Yasmin asked.

"We came to tell you about the school," Noam said, though he couldn't take his eyes off Yasmin's eyes. Bedu was right. She was beautiful like an angel.

"What school?"

"The school King Bedu started," Tamir added.

"Really," Yasmin said with great amusement. "King Bedu started a school? Well, please come in. I need to hear all about this."

NOAM WAS BACK in time for lunch, just as Bedu had asked.

"School on Monday, right?"

"Yes, Noam. You know that. Why?"

"Just checking."

"How was your ride with Tamir?"

"It was fun. Same classes? On Monday, I mean."

"Yes, Noam...same classes. Are you up to something?"

"Nothing."

"Noam!"

"Well, tomorrow Tamir and I are going to go visit some of the other children in town. Not everyone knows we have a school here."

"Okay, that sounds like a good idea. I'll come with you."

"No! I mean, um, it would be better if just Tamir and I talked with the other children. You know."

Bedu smiled. He *did* know.

"Okay. Well, good luck."

Monday came and, sure enough, nine more boys joined the crowd. Bedu's school now had thirty students. The language class with the widow went well, then the animal class with Bedu was always fun. The math class was the hardest, but all the children looked forward to the fourth class – the best class of the day – poetry.

Bedu finished his poetry presentation and was about to dismiss the class when there was a commotion in the street. All the boys stood up to see what was going on. Tamir and Noam knew *exactly* what was going on.

More than forty young girls – and their mothers – were following the "tree woman" down the middle of the street.

Bedu was speechless.

"Now, we're going to have our fifth class, King Bedu," Tamir said as the girls poured into the classroom beneath the canvas sails. They sat in the section to the right of the boys, just as their mothers had requested.

Yasmin walked to the front of the class. She was carrying a seedling in a large pot.

"Yasmin?" Bedu pressed.

"You didn't tell me you started a *school*. I thought you said you were a shepherd boy from Damascus?"

"Okay class, my name is Miss Yasmin and I'm going to be teaching you about the cedar trees that live up on our mountain in the forest of God..."

Her voice trickled off as Bedu was overcome with the sight of almost eighty children sitting under sails in his backyard school by the stables. Noam had never been prouder in his life.

There was no time to speak with Yasmin after class. She marched out and down the street with the girls and their mothers just as fast as she had arrived.

By the end of the week, twenty more girls joined the class and – where there are girls – a couple more dozen boys decided to learn math as well. Bedu's school was now overflowing with more than one hundred children.

The last day of class each week was always the worst day for the students. They wanted more.

"On Monday, we will all take a field trip for the day," Yasmin said as she closed the class. "All other classes will be cancelled on Monday, but just for Monday."

"Where are we going, Miss Yasmin?" a young girl asked.

"Up the mountain. To my house. Boys and girls, and of course all the mothers that want to come. We have one hundred cedars to plant on the mountainside. Each seedling will need almost the size of a ship to be planted in."

"How big do the cedars get?" a boy asked.

"As tall as you can imagine and as wide...well, as wide...as five Yasmin's and four-and-a-half Bedu's."

The children were amazed. Even though they lived in the foothills of the forest of God, few had ever seen them.

"We will meet at my house on the rocks. Follow the only road up. I'm sure your mothers have heard all about it – and me," Yasmin said as the children laughed.

Later that night, Noam was in bed asleep. Bedu went outside just to brush Atlas and check on Athena. The sheep were bedded down. The rams were a bit feisty.

Bedu lifted his eyes to the heavens. He recounted the four stars he was watching, the four stars that now had meaning for him. Working together with other people, they freed a little boy from a raging flood. He remembered the outcasts gathered all around him the morning after he fed them, a circle of protection from those who were neither wanted nor understood. He remembered the magical love he felt for Noam and Wali in Hebron and the words of The Speaker who said treat others like you want to be treated.

All these things worked together to change his life. And somehow, someway, Bedu was able to unleash the simple power of a school, and more than one hundred children would now start their own journeys.

By the end of the summer, young boys, and even some girls, were teaching their fathers how to breed sheep and start a business. The mothers added a class and taught the girls, and even some boys, how to weave the wool into garments they could sell. Merchants found new buyers for dyes and colors which brought the garments to life. The innkeeper added rooms to his hotel and hired the older boys to check guests in, collect their rent, and pay them back the appropriate amount of change. Almost all the children could read and write basic Aramaic. They made signs and put them up around the Bsharri District, advertising the weekly gathering in the town square where one and all could hear the captivating words of Bedu, the poet king.

And for the next one thousand years, maybe two, generations of admirers would walk the mountain land among one hundred new cedars in the forest of God.

Unleash: *When you unleash the power of new possibilities, it fuels your ability to change into something far greater.*

7

BEFORE THE NEW SCHOOL YEAR STARTED, THERE WAS SOMETHING BEDU KNEW HE JUST HAD TO DO.

He had to go home.

It would soon be a year since he left with five gold coins to replace his father's herd. He still wondered if his father somehow knew that he had stolen five more.

That seemed so long ago but it still nagged on Bedu's conscience. He prepared for the trip and packed a few things. He could make the ride easily in five days, though he figured Atlas might prefer four.

Bedu and Noam saddled up and road the mountain to Yasmin's house. There was no need to pull the horseshoe on the wooden door that was hung with iron hinges as Yasmin was already outside and ran to Noam, helped him off Athena, and gave him a big hug.

"How long will you be gone, Bedu?" she asked.

"School starts again in two weeks. I'll be back by then," he said as Noam ran up and kissed him goodbye on both cheeks. "Make Noam do chores. He knows how to work."

Noam and Yasmin laughed. "Don't worry about us, baba," Noam said.

Bedu turned around and waved several times as Atlas took him back down the mountain. Noam and Yasmin stood still in the doorway, frozen in time, as the rider dressed in black with a flowing black scarf tied around his forehead, disappeared.

AMIRA WAS UP tending the seven new sheep and four new goats on the hill by the pond above the house when she spotted a lone rider approaching at a fast speed.

She was immediately frightened and ran down to the house just as Yara looked out the window and saw him approaching as well.

"One rider, Abbas, he's coming quickly."

Abbas appeared from the other room and moved with urgency. He grabbed a knife and stuck it in the tied sash of the robe behind his back.

"You two stay in the house," he said as he went outside, past his mud and stone wall, and down to the dirty road where only a few dusty footprints had survived the last rain.

Atlas screeched to a stop in front of the man, then pranced around him in a circle as the rider tried to get control.

"I am Abbas, this is my house."

The rider pulled the black scarf from his forehead. His beard was full and dark, no longer like that of a boy.

"I am Bedu, baba...I am your son."

Abbas fell to the ground. His tears mixed with the dirt as Yara and Amira ran out of the house. Bedu jumped down from Atlas and ran to greet his mother who was crying herself.

The reunion meal was the happiest event Yara had ever cooked and Abbas could not stop pulling on Bedu's beard. They were amazed, relieved, overcome with joy that not only their son was alive, but that he had come home.

Bedu regaled them with stories from his adventure. The drowning boy near Jericho. The robbery on the road to Efrat and the strangers who took him in, nurtured him back to health, gave him work and three shekels of silver, and made him a new sheepskin satchel. He told them about the kabobs and the outcasts in Halhul. He told them about Wali, his youngest son and his wife, and of course, about Noam. He explained how Wali taught him the business of sheep breeding, gave him a line of credit, and the fever. He described the inheritance Wali gave him for raising Noam. He told them about Capernaum and the words of The Speaker. He told them about the school, his students, and the flock of sheep and rams that he already had.

And he told them about Yasmin, the tree woman, who had captured his heart in the cedars of the forest of God.

Yara grew silent and concerned.

"Bedu...Yasmin is the granddaughter of a king...she rode with a Persian army...she is royalty herself."

"I know, mama."

"Don't let your heart be broken, son. A woman like that is not dreaming of a shepherd boy from Damascus. You are wonderful. You will make a great husband. Just don't let your heart get too far ahead of your lips."

Bedu knew exactly what his mother was saying. She was wise, and probably right.

"I respect you, mama…I respect you, baba. You have taught me great things, things I still remember and things I teach my students even now."

"We love you, Bedu…we are so proud of all that you have done. Will you bring Noam here to live with us, too?" Abbas asked.

Bedu knew this would be difficult.

"Baba, my home is in Bsharri now. I bought a house there, I have students, and I have Noam…my son."

Yara got up and left the room, unable to hold back her sobs.

"Baba, I want you and mama and Amira to come with me…come live in my house in Bsharri. It is four times the size of our home here. My field is filled with sheep and rams. Let me take care of you now, baba. Let me be the son you raised."

"Is there snow?" Amira asked.

"Lots of snow…and Tamir."

"Who?"

"The shepherd boy who brought the sheep and goats. He told me you were cute," Bedu laughed.

"Cute? I hate boys," Amira said as she stormed out of the room. Though Bedu could see her brushing her hair and smiling in the hall.

"Son, this was my father's house, his fathers before him. It is mine now and will soon be yours. We can't leave. This is our home. Come home, son. This is who *we* are. This is who *you* are."

Bedu stood up. His mind was all confused. He walked out the front door, past the mud and stone wall and up to his favorite spot in the green grass by the pond. He was surrounded by seven new sheep and four new goats. Atlas was hanging out next to the camel in the lean-to stables.

Then she arrived.

She spoke to him in magical words that measured his thoughts in gold and pink hues of the setting sun. Flames of red and orange danced across the sky.

"From something we become nothing; and from nothing we become something. Dusty footsteps on winding roads of mud and stone lead to something, yet quickly leave behind nothing. When the sun rises, will seeds once planted rise for the harvest? Or must we wait? Why can't we enjoy today that which we planted yesterday? Patience. Like the deep roots of a cedar tree that once blew in the wind as but a seed, patience brings the strength and the shade. From the heights of great cedars, will we look back at dirty footsteps and realize that nothing…was *ever*…left behind."

Bedu felt the warm hand on his shoulder. Abbas sat next to him and they both stared at the sky. The silence between them lasted an eternity but ended softly and suddenly.

"You're right, Bedu…you are no longer this. You are so much more. But this is where I belong. This is where I will stay until I die. Go. Go be with your students, in your new home, with your new son, and your new flock. Make a life for yourself that is even better than ours."

Bedu buried his head in his father's chest and wept.

"I can't leave you, baba…I respect you too much."

"I know you do, and I respect you and all that you have accomplished. But it's because I respect you, and you I, that I must set you free to follow your heart. Just promise that you'll come home often to visit your mother. She worries."

They both laughed.

"Baba, I am asking you one thing. Just one thing. It's the only thing I will ever ask of you, I promise."

"What is it, Bedu?

"Don't tell me 'no', please…just say not yet. When the day becomes right, please come to me, baba."

Abbas smiled. "Very well, son…not yet."

Abbas got up and walked back into the house that was now lit with the same lanterns Bedu knew so well as a child. He laid his head back in the green grass and pondered the heavens above him. The five stars he had followed were lit brightly in formation, just as they had been for generations of eternity. But there in Damascus, he could see the sixth star. It meant respect to Bedu. Respect for his family, respect for his adventure, and respect for this one life which had given him so much opportunity.

R espect: *Paths you have traveled and people you have met, have all shaped who you are today. Respect that.*

8

BSHARRI DISTRICT WAS TRANSFORMED INTO A BUS-TLING VILLAGE OVER THE NEXT YEAR. Bedu's herd now numbered more than two hundred sheep and his rams were plenty.

Local shepherds saw incredible increases in the number of their flocks as well after their children came home from school and taught them how to breed and build a business.

The wool was harvested in amounts never seen before next to the sea. Bedu built a building at the end of the main street, a factory of sorts, where boys, girls and their mothers weaved the wool into fashionable garments.

Bsharri became a main intersection for merchant caravans. They would come to sell their dyes and inks and then buy the garments to sell in faraway lands.

And every Sunday – in the middle of the town square – Bedu would tell his stories, recite his poems – and the crowds, now numbering more than three hundred, would walk away with fuller hearts.

More beams and more sails were added to the school. Six classes were taught every day to more than one hundred and fifty students. Some children from nearby villages even walked to Bedu's school. All the classes were special, but there was always a noticeable increase of attention when it was time for the fifth class taught by Miss Yasmin, the tree woman.

There was so much commerce in town that the innkeeper added ten more rooms to his inn and three families started restaurants.

Bedu and Atlas made fewer trips up the mountain to see Yasmin, but Noam and Athena went up almost every day. Noam usually gave Yasmin a ride home after school.

"Do you want to come inside for a snack? I'm going to bake some fresh bread," Yasmin asked as Noam thought with his feet and beat her to the front wooden door with iron hinges. "I guess that's yes," Yasmin laughed as she tied Athena up in the stables.

"School will be out soon for the summer," Noam said with a hint of sadness.

"You love going to school, don't you?"

"I've never had so many friends. Friends are like a family. Now I have a large family," Noam said as he sat on the stool by the table as Yasmin rolled out the wheat flour, water and salt. "What kind of bread is that going to be, Yasmin?"

"Kita. My grandfather calls it chechebsa. His friends with very dark skin taught him how to make it."

"Do you miss him? Your grandfather?"

Yasmin reflected. "Yes, sometimes. But he is happy, and I am very happy. He lives up by the sea. Only a two-day ride from here. I'll probably go see him soon. Maybe you'll let me borrow Athena," she said with a sly smile.

"Do you have lots of friends here, Yasmin? Like I do?"

She laughed. "I'm not in school like you are, Noam. But yes, I have friends. But my best friends are the cedars that surround me. They are faithful and always happy."

"I think baba has a new friend," Noam said as he played with the flour.

"Bedu? Who? One of the merchants?"

"No. She walks her little brother to school every morning from one of the nearby villages. She stays all day then walks her brother back to the village after class. She likes to smile at baba. Baba says she is nice. Her father is a shepherd."

Yasmin suddenly started to pound the wheat flour, water and salt with extra vigor.

"Why do you have to hit the bread so hard, Yasmin?"

"It's a flatbread," she said pounding and pounding and pounding. "It must be very thin before I cook it in the pan."

The kita baked in a flash. Noam thought it was the best bread he had ever eaten.

"Aren't you going to eat any, Yasmin?"

She shook her head. "I'm not hungry anymore."

The next day, class ended, but unlike every other day, Yasmin stayed back to say good-bye to all the children as some walked home alone and others were gathered up by their mothers who sat in the shade behind the class each day. She saw the "smiling girl" and her little brother pause. They were not ready to leave with the others. "Smiling girl" started to walk toward Bedu just as Yasmin bolted ahead of her.

"Bedu," Yasmin said sternly.

"Yasmin, another great class today. You are teaching the children so many things," Bedu said as he waved to several of the children leaving in the street.

The woman and her little brother left quickly.

"What is wrong with you?" Yasmin demanded.

Bedu fell silent and was confused, but he knew enough to know that she was angry. He recalled the same look and the same tone from his mother. He remembered his father, Abbas, clearing out of the house to pick wildflowers whenever Yara got angry.

"What have I done to anger you, Yasmin? Please tell me."

"What have you done?" Yasmin's eyes flared and flashed. She kicked some dirt, spun around instantly, and jumped up on Athena where Noam waited patiently.

Yasmin pushed her heels into Athena who took off on a gallop as Noam turned back to wave goodbye to Bedu.

Bedu waved back, his mouth still agape.

Yasmin got off Athena quickly and marched to the front of the house. She opened – then slammed – the wooden door that hung on iron hinges.

Noam and Athena turned and walked home.

Bedu was cooking some kabobs for dinner when Noam walked in. Cheese and milk were already placed by each of their plates on the table. Noam sat down on the bench and reached for the cheese.

"Did you wash?" Bedu asked without even turning around from the lamb kabobs he was cooking. Noam got up and poured water over his hands and down into the basin, then sat back down. "Thank you."

Hundreds of people gathered in the town square for Sunday's performance. Bedu was now inviting three students each Sunday to perform with him. The first girl had already started telling her poetic story when Bedu noticed Noam and Athena walking up to the back of the crowd. Yasmin was not with them.

She didn't come.

Yasmin *never* missed a Sunday performance. Noam seemed sad.

The audience was disappointed when Bedu closed the show and apologized for not performing himself. He told them that his throat was sore from a full week of school but promised he would be back next week.

Bedu had never missed performing on a Sunday afternoon either.

As the crowd dispersed, Noam came up to him.

"Are you okay, baba? I didn't know you were sick."

"I'm fine, Noam. Just tired. Are you still going to play with Tamir today?"

Noam perked up. "Yes, his mother asked if I could have dinner with them. Can I, baba?"

Bedu smiled. "Of course. Be sure to wash and only start eating after Tamir's father and mother have started eating."

"Yes, baba. Are you going home to eat alone?"

"No, I think Atlas and I will go for a ride today."

Noam grew sad and dropped his head slightly. "Out to the village? To the see the smiling girl?"

Bedu was confused. "Village? Smiling -. No. I think we will ride up the mountain and see the cedars."

Noam was elated and gave Bedu a hug before he grabbed Athena's reins and led her down the main street toward the inn.

Bedu pulled the horseshoe back three times.

Nothing.

He pulled it back three more times.

Still nothing.

He assumed she was inside, saw him ride up, and wanted nothing to do with him.

His mother's words echoed in his mind: "Yasmin is the grand-daughter of a king...she rode with a Persian army...she is royalty herself. Don't let your heart be broken, son. A woman like that is not dreaming of a shepherd boy from Damascus. You are wonderful. You will make a great husband. Just don't let your heart get too far ahead of your lips."

Dejected, Bedu walked around to the other side of the house, away from the stables. He wanted to see the cedars, maybe walk among them, before he rode down the mountain. He walked higher and higher, reaching out his hand to caress the trunks of the mighty cedars as he passed by. He walked straight on a path that led to the plateau, the place where the sea was visible on the distant horizon.

She was there.

Leaning against a tree.

He was about to leave when he heard her soft cries. She was upset.

He walked over quietly, checking each step to make sure no twigs or branches would give him away.

He sat down. Next to Yasmin. He said not a word.

"I...I thought...I thought maybe, somehow...just maybe... that you found me to be special. That maybe you could love me," she said through tears as she buried her face in her sleeves.

Bedu sat back against the tree. His eyes flared in disbelief. He swallowed hard.

"Yasmin...I loved you the moment I saw you get up from the wagon and help King Melchior out of the straw. I rode for days from Hebron to Bsharri to see you...to check on you. And I have loved you every day since. Your smile measures the gold and pink hues of the setting sun. Your heart flames the red and orange that dance across my sky. Your spirit is my morning dawn and your strength becomes the hours in my day. I have loved you every minute since I first saw you." Bedu stopped. Tears were flowing down his cheeks now, too. "And yet, I know that you will never be mine."

Yasmin lifted her head.

"Your grandfather is a king. You were guided by your father's army who built you this great house. You have been in school since you were a child and you already know more than I could ever possibly learn." Yasmin turned to look at him. Their faces were closer than they had ever been. "You are a princess, Yasmin...and I am just a shepherd boy from Damascus."

Yasmin stood up. She shook her head. Bedu feared another round of wrath was coming his way from her lips.

"Do you see servants around me, Bedu? Do you see people cooking my meals? Does a chariot bring me to school every morning? Do the children of Bsharri bow to me each day? No. But, you look at me and judge me. You have decided who I am. You have decided what I want. And you have decided who I will forever be."

"But my mother said -." Yasmin waved him off.

"Have you ever asked me what I want? Have you ever bothered to look into my heart? Do you even care who I am? Or are you blinded by an army, my grandfather's treasure, and my new house?"

"But -."

Yasmin walked close and kneeled in front of Bedu who leaned back against the trunk of a great cedar overlooking the sea.

"Yes, you were once a shepherd boy from Damascus. That is what you *did*. But that's not even close to who you *were*. Even in Damascus, you weren't just a shepherd boy. Look at you Bedu. Have you ever looked at yourself to see who you have become? You are a man who saved a boy near Jericho. You were a beaten man who recovered in the home of strangers after losing everything. And even though you earned some shekels of silver, you gave it all away to feed outcasts who had nothing. You are the man who helped a cousin, learned a business, and adopted a young boy with only the love a father could have for a son. You are the man who started a school, taught boys and girls how to build a business and breed sheep. You are the man who taught them that weaving garments was a better way than just selling wool. And you are the man I have loved since the moment I helped my grandfather get down from a bed of straw in a wagon. And still, you say you are *just* a shepherd boy from Damascus..."

Bedu didn't know what to say.

"You were cared for by one hundred and thirty-two soldiers. Mighty warriors. Every one of them would kill the other just to be your husband."

Yasmin smiled. "And do you see them now? Are they here? Hiding in the forest of God?" Yasmin screamed. "HELP...HELP ME..." The forest was silent. "Or am I here, alone with you?"

Yasmin reached out and took Bedu's hand.

"I once heard a poet say these words. I hoped he was talking about me. 'From something…we become nothing; and from nothing…we become something. Dusty footsteps on winding roads of mud and stone lead to something, yet quickly leave nothing behind. When the sun rises, will seeds once planted rise for the harvest? Or must we wait another day? Why can't we enjoy today that which we planted only yesterday? Patience. Like the deep roots of a cedar tree that once blew in the wind as but a seed, patience brings us the strength of the trunk for our families and the shade of the branches to cover our worry. From the heights of great cedars, will we look back at dirty footsteps and realize that nothing…was ever left behind.'"

"You remembered?"

"Bedu…nothing is ever left behind, the good or the bad. It's who we are. Being a shepherd boy from Damascus is a great part of who you are today. Having a family such as yours is a great part of who you are today. But you have also planted seeds that are rising for harvest. Seeds like a school, businesses, a young boy named Noam, and a Persian girl named Yasmin. Yet, you look back at one picture… one moment in time…and say *that's* who you are. It's not, Bedu. It's not the whole picture. There's so much more."

Bedu leaned forward and kissed Yasmin on the lips. He had never kissed a woman other than his mother. He felt things he had never felt before.

"Would a tree woman from Persia marry a shepherd boy from Damascus?"

Yasmin smiled.

"If he asked her, he would know that answer."

The next morning, Bedu was packed, the sheepskin satchel draped around his neck and shoulder. His black riding clothes and scarf were in place. Atlas was more than ready for the two-day ride to Aabdeh, though Atlas might prefer one.

"Take your time, baba. I'll be fine here with Miss Yasmin," Noam said as he clutched her leg.

"You just like her cooking better than mine," Bedu answered as Yasmin laughed.

"Tell my grandfather I love him, Bedu. And be careful."

With a wave, Atlas was off. Bedu didn't have time to turn around and wave but knew they were still standing in the doorway. In his mind's eye, they would forever be frozen in time.

Bedu and Atlas rode briskly past Karm Sedah to Zgharta, past Tripoli and up the coast to Aabdeh. King Melchior's house was exactly where Yasmin said it would be. It was a beautiful stone and wood home with open windows overlooking the Mediterranean Sea below. White and blue curtains danced in the breeze that blew up from the sands and rocks below.

Four guards moved to the road in front of Bedu as Atlas approached.

"I come from Bsharri with a message from King Melchior's granddaughter, Yasmin."

"Who are you?"

"I am Bedu."

"The shepherd boy from Damascus?"

Bedu nodded. The guards were quite surprised. Bedu dismounted and a servant ran over to take the reins. Atlas was soon enjoying fresh water and oats as his coat was brushed out in luxury accommodations.

One of the guards led him around the side of the house over a perfectly laid porch, paved with precious granite and marble. The king was lounging in a chair and wore a flowing robe. Two cups for chai were on the table by his side as he read the fading ink on ancient papers.

"I knew I would see you again, Bedu," the king said without looking up. The guard left as Bedu sat down. "Tea?"

Bedu reached over and poured some chai in the second cup.

"Were you expecting someone else, King Melchior?" Bedu asked.

"No. Just you."

"How did you know?"

The Magi smiled. "The stars, my son. The stars have meaning. They told me you would be coming."

"Did they say why?" Bedu asked with a sly smile.

King Melchior laughed.

"How was your journey, Bedu? Did you replace your father's flock? Did you find the stars? The seventh one, too?"

"Not the seventh, King Melchior. I haven't seen that one. But still I look. Every night."

For the next several hours, Bedu told King Melchior about his journey. There was the collaboration with six strangers in a village near Jericho as the muddy flood waters of the Jordan River tried to take a young boy from his mother. It was on the road to Efrat that all his gold coins were stolen, and his body was beaten unconscious. But it was the love and compassion of two kind people who took him home, nurtured him back to health, and even gave him work for a few shekels of silver. King Melchior loved his sheepskin satchel.

Bedu had lost everything again.

He told him about the woman with sores on her face and hands. She had asked for food for her children as Bedu pretended to sleep. Finally, he found his true self, marched past the gates, and brought food back for all who were hungry. Bedu described the scene in the morning when he was surrounded by outcasts who had formed a circle of protection around him throughout the night.

This time, Bedu had given away freely all that he had. The king seemed pleased. Bedu understood people better, especially outcasts.

King Melchior was thrilled that he found Wali, the cousin of Abbas, but was sad to learn that his youngest son had succumbed to the fever. His face glowed with excitement as he heard about Noam, learning the business of breeding sheep, and the addition of Atlas and Athena to his growing family.

Clearly, Bedu had learned to love Noam as his own son.

Bedu took great pride in telling the king that he left Hebron and rode for days to check on Yasmin in the winter as he had promised. The king nodded his pleasure.

The school, the size of his herd, the businesses and the factory where students would weave the wool into fine garments, all gave the king great pleasure. He nodded in satisfaction. The king was proud of Yasmin for teaching such a great class and restoring the forest of God for future generations.

"But I'm not surprised," the king said. "I knew you would unleash great ideas and ambitions to serve others."

Bedu grew slightly sadder as he described his trip back home to see Abbas, Yara and Amira. He had such great respect for his father and their family traditions. He told the king of wanting his family to come live with him. His father had said no, but Bedu negotiated a "not yet" before he left.

Hours passed.

Darkness was now covering the sea. The servants cleared the food from the table and started a small fire to keep the king warm.

"I'm ninety-four now, Bedu...my bones get colder than they did when I was a young man."

"I like the fire," Bedu said as they looked out over the darkened sea. The only sounds were waves hitting the rocks below and wood yielding to the fire to give heat.

"The problem with the warmth of the fire is that I can't see the stars until the flames retreat and the embers glow. Then I can find meaning. I must be patient."

Bedu reached for his satchel and pulled it close. He opened it to the hidden compartment and started to pull out gold coins. Within seconds, fifty gold coins were on the table next to King Melchior's chair.

"King...I beg that you forgive me."

"Forgive you for what, Bedu?"

"In Damascus, when you visited my father...I took five gold coins from your trunk and put them in the pocket of my robe. I stole from you, King Melchior. I have been ashamed since that night."

"And these?"

"I return ten times what I took from you and beg that you forgive me."

King Melchior looked over at the coins. He nodded his head.

"Why did you take them, son?"

Bedu grew silent. He thought. He had never really asked himself that question. It was something he just did, without thinking really.

"I don't...I don't really know, king."

King Melchior looked over and smiled.

"Sure, you do, son. Tell me."

"Your arrival was...unexpected. Baba was not a wealthy man. We were eating bone soup and waiting desperately for the harvest. We were already afraid that we might have to eat one of the goats, just to get by."

"And then?"

"And then you arrived...with an army. I had never even heard of you before. And suddenly, my father told me to get behind the seven sheep and four goats and drive them into the slaughtering pen. I'm a shepherd, not a butcher. He gave you everything he had. I was angry."

"And you wanted those coins to give it all back to your father."

Bedu nodded.

"Why would your father do that, Bedu? He had a wife, two children. As you say, he was already out of food and had little. Why would he give everything he still had just to feed an army and an old Magi for one night?"

Bedu didn't speak. He didn't have an answer for that, nor had he ever contemplated it before.

"Because that's...who...he *is*, son. That's who he is. He is a man of great love. I knew that when I first met him as a boy thirty-two years ago, and I found the same man in Damascus when we were hungry. But you couldn't see *that* man, could you? You wondered what he would do to survive. I knew he would survive because of who he is. 'Be' always *guides* 'do' if you have values, Bedu. If you know what is truly important."

A tear streaked down Bedu's face.

"And I was a man who would do such an evil thing as steal from my father's friend," Bedu said in shame. "That is who *I* am."

"Not exactly," King Melchior said after he let Bedu squirm for a minute or two.

"What do you mean?"

"You took the coins, I assume, to replenish all that your father had given away."

Bedu nodded.

"But in doing so, you took away the power of the gift that you didn't know I planned to give. I knew Abbas had nothing. I gave him five gold coins which would give him more than he had ever had before. You didn't steal five coins from me, Bedu. You stole your father's blessing."

Bedu understood. The king was very wise.

"And then you lost my gift and your father's blessing on the road to Efrat."

Bedu was silent. This was not going well at all. It would have been far better if the king was just angry and accepted the repayment with interest.

"I knew," the king said after an uncomfortable pause.

"Knew what, King Melchior?"

"Javad, the commander of the army, saw you take the coins. He told me."

"Why didn't you stop me then?"

"And learn what? Learn that you got caught stealing, so you could learn how *not* to get caught the next time? That would be of no use for a shepherd boy from Damascus. Your father agreed with me."

"My father? You told him that I stole the coins from you?"

Bedu was mortified.

"Bedu, when I was a child, I stole a knife from my father. He acted as though he had misplaced it. But he knew. That night at dinner, mother put food down – rabbits – for father, herself, my sister and my brother. But there was no food for me. I was sad. I looked to my mother, but she would not look at my eyes. I knew there was no point in asking her. Father didn't wait. 'Where is your food, son?' he asked. I was confused. 'I think you have a new knife which certainly means now that you know how to catch a rabbit, skin it, and cook it for yourself.' I left the table, went to my room, and brought him his knife in shame. 'That's not mine. That's your knife. I hope you have good luck with the rabbits. You must be very hungry.'"

"What happened?"

"What happened is I didn't eat for four days…until I learned to use that knife…until I learned to hunt rabbits… and until mother taught me how to cook one. Father could have punished me for what I had done. Yes, I deserved it. But then I would not have learned how to use that knife and care for myself. I missed four days of meals then…but I have never been hungry since."

"You're a wise man, King Melchior."

"I'm not a king," he answered as they both laughed. "Sometimes it is better to let those who have stumbled endure their own consequences. That's how we learn. That's how we grow."

Bedu and King Melchior tipped their heads back and began to admire the stars above them as orange and red embers warmed from below.

"Well, are you going to ask me or not?" King Melchior finally pressed.

Bedu knew he knew. Perhaps he read it in the stars.

"Do you love her, Bedu?"

"More than the sands in the sea, Magi."

"Will you be her partner in this journey and not her master? Yasmin will not put up with a master. Trust the old man on that one, son."

Bedu laughed heartily.

"I will be her partner."

"Will you walk with her hand in hand through the forest of God all the days of her life?"

"I promise."

King Melchior clapped his hands and a servant came running. He bowed down as the king whispered in his ear, then left as fast as he had arrived.

The servant returned with a small box and gave it to King Melchior who opened it carefully. He reached in and pulled out a small piece of silk, that was knotted up in a ball tied with a leather lace.

"Give this to Yasmin. It's the ring her father, my son, gave to Yasmin's mother on their wedding day. She was the most beautiful woman I had ever seen. Well, until I held Yasmin as a baby. Yasmin will know she has my blessing when she sees this."

Bedu took the silk and carefully put it in the hidden pocket inside his satchel.

They both sat in silence, inhaling the beauty of the night sky and the stars that reflected on the sea.

"There it is, Bedu. Your seventh star. See it? You have evolved from a shepherd boy in Damascus to become a great, tender and wise man who runs businesses and a school. You have changed and – most of all – you were *willing* to change. And now you will marry a princess."

Bedu slapped his knee. "I knew you were a king."

King Melchior started to sit up.

"Anything else from your journey, Bedu, that you wish to tell me? I am weary now and must take my rest."

Bedu took his hand and pulled him to his feet.

"I will tell you about The Speaker in the morning, before I leave. Now you should rest."

King Melchior sat back down.

"The Speaker?"

"It can wait until morning, king."

"Tell me now, Bedu. Tomorrow is never guaranteed, but today is."

"Well, Noam and I had pushed hard for several days in our travels from Hebron to Bsharri, so we camped out by the Sea of Galilee. Near Capernaum. Suddenly, a great crowd of people began to arrive. They sat on blankets everywhere. There were hundreds of people, King Melchior…I've never seen so many people."

"Go on."

"Then this man climbed up the rocks and began to speak to the crowds. His voice echoed off the rocks in the hills and over the water of Galilee. I could hear him perfectly."

"What did The Speaker say, Bedu?"

"Wonderful things. Beautiful things. Things that were so simple to understand but so deep they could fill your heart."

"Things like what, my son?"

"Blessed are the poor in spirit…Blessed are the meek, for they shall be comforted…blessed are they that mourn, for they shall be comforted…blessed are they that hunger and thirst after justice for they shall have their fill. Blessed are the merciful for they shall obtain it…blessed are the clean of heart. Blessed are the peacemakers for they shall be called children of God…"

King Melchior's face was illuminated as he lifted his eyes to the sky.

"Eight? Were there eight things he said?"

"Yes, I think so. I don't remember all of them. Then he closed with 'Treat others the way you wish to be treated.' I have tried to live my life like that, King Melchior, I really have."

"How old of a man was The Speaker?" the king asked.

"I don't know for sure. We were not that close, but we could hear him clearly. Older than me but much younger than my father. Maybe thirty. I don't know."

King Melchior's eyes closed softly, seemingly fixed on one star in the heavens that he imagined was brighter than all the others.

"You have given me the greatest gift of all, Bedu. You have given me the eighth star. Look. Now I can see it," the king said though his eyes were still closed.

In the morning, King Melchior walked out to the stables where the servants had Atlas ready for the trip home. Bedu noticed the large pouch that was tied to the back of his saddle.

"What's this?" Bedu asked.

"A wedding gift for you and Yasmin. Open it when you marry."

"But King Melchior, surely you plan to come to our wedding. It will be in Bsharri, in the town square on the first Saturday in August."

King Melchior touched Bedu's shoulder.

"I am too old for such a journey anymore, Bedu. I wish you well, now go with my blessing."

Evolve: *When you are willing to change, become better and serve others, a new path for living grows beneath you.*

9

THE ENERGY IN BSHARRI DISTRICT WAS LIKE LIGHTNING.

The crowds were gathering, and excitement filled the air. Merchant caravans from all parts of the world had arrived and set up camps in the fields nearby. A gazebo was built in the center of the town square where Bedu usually performed. Fresh flowers and flowing ribbons adorned the posts and columns.

Yasmin and the women were down at the inn. They had weaved the most beautiful gown for her to wear out of the wool from Bedu's sheep. The merchants brought the perfect blue dye she wanted from Persia and she was thrilled.

Noam and his friends paced nervously at the back of the street. Every few seconds, Tamir asked him if he still had the silk bundle tied with a leather lace. Noam showed it each time, just to make sure it had not been lost.

Bedu sat atop of Atlas waiting near his home. He chose to wear the black riding outfit that Wali had given him. It had belonged to his youngest son. He breathed deeply to take it all in. The flock. The factory. The new rooms at the inn. The gazebo. The magical house on the mountain. The forest of God. And his bride to be, Yasmin.

The sky didn't disappoint him. Yasmin had picked the day, but he had picked the magic hour when the gold and pink hues of the setting sun would unleash the flames of red and orange that danced across the sky to celebrate their wedding.

On cue, the boys in Bedu's school started a singular beat in unison on their ten drums.

The crowd stopped their conversation and edged in closer to the gazebo. Atlas began to walk. The Arabian lifted his legs higher and higher, as though he was marching. Stately he went, as each step matched the beat of the ten drums. If it were not a wedding, most would run in fear of an impending war and an approaching army.

Yasmin and the women heard the drums. She walked out of the inn looking as elegant as a princess should. The women helped her up into the carriage and Athena started her march to the center of the town where Atlas and Bedu now waited.

The crowd turned to see Yasmin long before she came around the corner.

Bedu waited.

His bride was drawing closer.

Atlas and Athena met nose to nose in the center of town. Bedu got down and handed the reins to Tamir as he went to the side of the carriage, offered his hand, and helped Yasmin to the street.

She was beautiful. Bedu had never seen such beauty.

Hand in hand, smiles beaming across their faces, the crowd parted to form a center aisle and Yasmin and Bedu walked to the steps leading up to the gazebo.

A young boy gasped.

"Look!" he screamed as he pointed up to the hills in the east leading down into Bsharri. Lanterns were ablaze, horses and wagons were approaching.

"It's an army," screamed another.

Some started to scatter but Bedu lifted his hands to calm them. He whispered into Yasmin's ear.

"What do you think?"

"Looks like about one hundred and thirty-two warriors," she said with a smile.

"I thought so, too…and some wagons."

The army pulled up as the ceremony stopped even before it began.

Atop his Arabian, Javad announced their arrival.

"I present King Melchior, grandfather of the princess."

The crowd was hushed. They had not expected the arrival of a king.

Yasmin pulled Bedu by the hand as they both walked quickly to the wagon where the old man was riding in the straw.

Bedu steadied King Melchior and helped him down.

"We're not too late, are we?" he said with a wink.

"Grandfather! I am so happy you came."

"Take me to a chair, Yasmin. It's been a long ride for an old man. I want to be in the front row."

Yasmin led the way until King Melchior stopped and turned back to Bedu.

"Son, please go get my packages out of the last wagon."

"More gifts?" Bedu asked but the king had already turned and sat down.

Bedu did as instructed. He passed through the crowds then one hundred and thirty-two soldiers as he went to the back and over to the last wagon.

He burst into uncontrollable tears.

He bent over with sobs.

"Baba...mama...Amira. I had no idea. I thought -."

"I said 'not yet' son. Besides, your mother heard you will have a large empty house tomorrow."

Bedu sobbed in the arms of his father and mother as Tamir walked over to lead Amira to the ceremony.

Tamir seemed very pleased.

The harps and flutes began to play as Bedu ushered his mother to the front row opposite King Melchior. Abbas followed behind in his dusty and dirty shepherd's robe.

When the ceremony was over, the crowd cheered Bedu and Yasmin as they got back into her carriage. Atlas was tied proudly behind. Yasmin admired her special ring and winked at Noam for doing such a great job protecting it. As the carriage started to pull away from the town center and back to the inn, one of the little merchant boys, a stranger to Bsharri who was only passing through with his father's caravan, walked up to King Melchior and tugged on his fine robe.

The old man looked down and smiled.

"Who *are* they, king?" he asked as the carriage disappeared around the corner.

"That's Bedu...Bedouin boy, poet king...and his princess Yasmin."

KING MELCHIOR DIED twenty-two years later in the Kingdom of Armenia when he was one hundred and sixteen years old.

But that was not the end of the meaning he found in his stars.

For the next two thousand years, people from all over the world traveled to Bsharri District. The schools numbered many, and the garment shops and factories flourished. Hotels, restaurants and shops were plentiful.

All had come to see the forest of God.

They walked among the giant cedars and paused beneath majestic branches. The trunks still measured five Yasmin's and four-and-a-half Bedu's.

And all these cedars had been planted in love by the tree woman so very long ago.

And when they listened closely, they could still hear the singular beats of ten drums in unison, flutes and harps announcing the arrival of a new marriage, the hoof-beats of a Persian army, the joy from a great wedding feast and poetic words echoing in the town square, beneath the roof of a Gazebo.

Yes, they could still hear Bedu...Bedouin Boy and Poet King.

Forever.

The Beginning

A FINAL WORD FROM THE AUTHOR...

Through the eyes of Bedu, a shepherd boy from Damascus, we discover the two words that govern the universe. These words guide our personal lives, our businesses, organizations and great institutions. They even guide militaries.

"Be" and "do."

Some people define who they are by what they do.

Others determine what they do, only so long as it's in harmony with who they truly are.

When the eulogies of our lives are written, will they read our résumés and talk about what we did and accomplished in life (do), or will they speak to who we were as people and how we treated others with love, compassion, and respect (be)?

Corporations, businesses, organizations and militaries are really no different than individual people. Those who tend to these large flocks are sometimes shepherds who lead from the front…they protect and guide their people to greener pastures and cool water. Others are butchers who get behind their flocks yelling and screaming and driving them, ultimately, to slaughter.

Who we are, dictates what we do, and how we do it.

And what we do, reflects who we are.

A corporation has a "be" and it's called culture. The products and services and tasks performed are the "do." How we approach quality, customer service and treat our employees is the "be" that defines an organization's culture.

Without great culture, there can be no great products or services. Culture is not a "light switch" event. It's a journey.

King Melchior used his wisdom to send Bedu out on a journey to find seven stars. In the process, Bedu found himself.

Shouldn't we all do that?

Colonel David W. Sutherland

U.S. Army, Retired

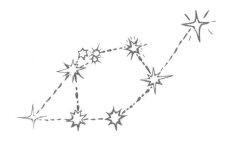

Collaborate: *Work together as a team and transform the impossible, to the possible.*

Understanding: *Realize you're not alone. Have empathy for those in need and turn nothing into something.*

Leadership: *When leaders love beyond self, life replaces emptiness and indecision with fulfillment and purpose.*

Treat: *Treat people – all people – well, no matter their station or position in life, and they will treat you well.*

Unleash: *When you unleash the power of new possibilities it fuels your ability to change into something far greater.*

Respect: *Paths you have traveled and people you have met, have all shaped who you are today. Respect that.*

Evolve: *When you are willing to change, become better and serve others, a new path for living grows beneath you.*

ABOUT THE AUTHORS...

COLONEL DAVID W. SUTHERLAND (US ARMY, RETIRED), was one of 13 Brigade Commanders during "surge" operations in the Iraq War. He culminated his military service as the Special Assistant to the Chairman of the Joint Chiefs of Staff with principle focus on Warrior and Family Support. He is respected not only by those he served with but by those he served for. He is recognized for his courage on and off the battlefield and is a fierce advocate for our service members, military veterans, their families, and the families of our fallen.

Following his 29 years of service, Colonel Sutherland has consulted with many corporations, nonprofits and government entities on the topics of leadership and organizational culture. He is also a nationally recognized speaker and vocal advocate for transformational change that is driven by visionary, ethical and engaged leaders.

He and his team at the Sutherland Partnership have developed tools to quantify what is happening inside specific corporations regarding culture (both positive and negative) and helps identify new ways to manage and enhance performance. He believes, from his experiences on the battlefield, that building a successful culture by informed leaders has become one of the most significant sources of competitive advantage and brand differentiation in business today. Culture is a fundamental driver of operational and individual performance as well as innovation, execution and overall company success.

 PAUL MCKELLIPS served under COL Sutherland during the Iraq War. "Pablo" and "Suds" are friends for life.

"In the spirit of *The Defense of Duffer's Drift* and *A Message to Garcia*, this simple tale offers profound insights on leadership and living with a purpose. For years, travelers relied on stars to guide their journey, and Bedu follows the stars to transform from what he 'does' to become who he is truly meant to 'be.' Everyone should take this journey."

—*Timothy M. Karcher, Colonel, U.S. Army (Retired), Leadership Consultant*

"A young tender of a small flock of sheep and goats – with a flair for effective communication – sets out to buy some replacement animals. His journey is fraught with seemingly insurmountable challenges and tough decisions, each unique but each important in different ways.

The authors draw on real-life experiences few of us will ever encounter, to spin a simple tale that offers aspiring leaders some compelling advice and guidance for their own journeys.

Bedu, in addition to courage, persistence, empathy and patience, shows others the power of self-reflection...and the results that follow. This powerful storytelling is a quick and worthwhile read for those on their own journey to confirm *who they are* and *who they can be*. *Bedu* is a really well-written and entertaining story."

—*Don Allard, President, AFI-NTX, LLC*

"Sometimes a 'back to the basics' reminder is needed to realign personal or team performance. *Bedu: Bedouin Boy, Poet King* is a fast-paced, compelling and delightful tale that reveals the seven foundational stars for successful business culture. But it's not just a business book! From teenagers to mid-life career changers; from the administrative assistant to the CEO; there's something for everyone in *Bedu*. This could be the most important two hours you've ever invested."

—*Robert S. Bahlman,*
Former Chief Financial Officer , Midwest Airlines

The Sutherland Partnership
P.O. Box 7313
Alexandria, VA 22307

For speaking engagements or general information, please call:
571-418-3041

info@sutherlandpartnership.com

SutherlandPartnership.com